D0403655

HIGH HURDLES

Class Act

LAURAINE SNELLING

BETHANY HOUSE PUBLISHERS
MINNEAPOLIS, MINNESOTA 55438

Published by Bethany House Publishers
A Ministry of Bethany Fellowship International
11400 Hampshire Avenue South
Minneapolis, Minnesota 55438
www.bethanyhouse.com

Printed in the United States of America by
Bethany Press International, Minneapolis, Minnesota 55438

Library of Congress Cataloging-in-Publication Data

Snelling, Lauraine.
    Class act / by Lauraine Snelling.
        p. cm. — (High hurdles ; bk. 10)
Summary: With the support of her family and friends, DJ undertakes
the long and difficult process of recovery from the serious burns she
received while saving horses from a deadly fire, but she is afraid she
may never ride again.
    ISBN 0–7642–2038–1 (pbk.)
    [1. Burns and scalds—Patients—Rehabilitation—Fiction.
2. Horses—Fiction. 3. Family life—Fiction. 4. Christian life—
Fiction.] I. Title.
    PZ7.S677 Cj 2000
    [Fic]—dc21

00–008441

To all those at Eagle One,
may you fly high and far.

LAURAINE SNELLING fell in love with horses by age five and never outgrew them. Her first pony, Polly, deserves a book of her own. Then there was Silver; Kit—who could easily have won the award for being the most ornery horse alive; a filly named Lisa; an asthmatic registered Quarter Horse called Rowdy; and Cimeron, who belonged to Lauraine's daughter, Marie. It is Cimeron who stars in *Tragedy on the Toutle*, Lauraine's first horse novel. All of the horses were characters, and all have joined the legions of horses who now live only in memory.

While there are no horses in Lauraine's life at the moment, she finds horses to hug in her research, and she dreams, like many of you, of owning one or three again. Perhaps a Percheron, a Peruvian Paso, a . . . well, you get the picture.

Lauraine lives in California with her husband, Wayne, basset hound, Woofer, and cockatiel, Bidley. Her two sons are grown and have dogs of their own; Lauraine and Wayne often dog-sit for their golden retriever granddogs. Besides writing, reading is one of her favorite pastimes.

1

WILL I EVER RIDE AGAIN? Darla Jean Randall stared out her hospital window at the early-September sun.

Of course you will. Don't be a boob. You can't let a little fire get you down.

But it wasn't just a little fire. The voices argued back and forth in her head, sometimes so loudly she couldn't feel the pain in her hands.

"Darla Jean?" The nurse stopped at the foot of her bed.

"My name is DJ." She knew Gran would give her that I'm-disappointed-in-you look if she heard a response like that, but why couldn't they get her name straight? She unclenched her jaw and attempted a smile. "Please call me DJ. Only my mother and grandmother call me Darla Jean." There, that sounded a bit better.

"Sorry. Here, let me fix that on your chart and the tag on your bed. We at least ought to be able to get your name right." The young woman wearing kittens all over her shirt corrected the chart and tag before coming closer to stand at DJ's side. "Okay, DJ, my name is Karen. I've been on vacation, but now I'll be your regular nurse. I hear you're our local heroine."

DJ shrugged. That's what several newspapers had called her when she saved a bunch of horses from a fire at Rancho de Equus horse park almost two weeks earlier. Good thing someone found her lying on the barn floor after she'd been clunked on the head trying to get another horse out or—

"How's your horse doing?" Karen broke into DJ's thoughts.

"Okay. My father has him back at his ranch in Santa Rosa." When DJ closed her eyes, she could still hear Herndon screaming in fear.

"We'll get you riding again, DJ." Karen's voice softened. "I can understand how much you love horses because I do, too. I never got as far as you have, though."

"Do you jump?"

"Nope, dressage. But I jumped some when I was younger." Karen finished injecting the pain medication into the IV drip.

"You don't anymore?"

"No horse now. One of these days I'll have one again." Karen glanced at her watch. "I hate to be the one to do this, but they're ready for you down in therapy."

DJ gritted her teeth and fought the tears that threatened to brim over. "Do I have to?" Every day they scrubbed the dead tissue off the burns on her hands. One time she had fainted. If only that would happen every time. Nothing in her entire life had ever hurt so much, not even the burns after the fire. But then, she'd been unconscious for several days and didn't remember anything. They'd stapled artificial skin over the burned tissue to help new skin grow faster while she was unconscious, too.

"Sorry. I wish there were another way, but we want to make sure your hands heal properly." The look in Karen's eyes said as much as the words. "You don't have to be tough, you know. Scream all you want."

I hate to be a sissy. God, please help me. I can't do this again. "Ah, is my grandmother here yet?"

"I can check after I get you down there."

"Can you check now, please?" Having to ask for every little thing made DJ want to run screaming down the hall. Since she still got dizzy when she stood up, they wouldn't even let her out of bed without someone standing by. Once, in the middle of the night, she nearly wet the bed when the nurse didn't get there in time. One thing was for sure—there was no way she'd ever be a nurse or doctor or medical anything.

She watched as the nurse left the room, the soles of her shoes squeaking on the highly polished floor. *Gran, please be here. I need you to pray for me.*

"Sorry, no one in the waiting room." Karen pushed a wheelchair next to the bed and set the brakes. "You need help getting into our speed-mobile here?"

DJ held her bandaged hands in the air and scooted her rear over to the side of the bed, bracing herself on her elbows. She sat upright and paused to make sure her head stayed in one place before swinging her legs over the sides. Even that extra bit made her close her eyes to stop the window from tilting.

"Easy, now." Karen laid a restraining hand on DJ's upper arm. "Has the room stopped spinning yet?"

"I . . . I think so." DJ opened her eyes and swallowed.

"Okay, lean on me and we'll keep you off the floor." Together they got DJ situated in the wheelchair, and Karen flipped the footrests into place. "You all right?"

"Um . . ." DJ propped her elbows on the arms of the chair. Her stomach tied up in knots and her hands shook, even in all the bandages. One second she felt cold, the other steaming hot. *Gran, where are you?*

By the time they arrived at the treatment room, she kept swallowing to keep from throwing up. Someone in treatment screamed. DJ flinched. *Oh, God, please, I can't do this again. I can't.*

"Darla Jean, sweetheart." Gran's voice drenched her in a cooling, life-giving shower.

Karen stopped before the doors and waited as Gran hurried down the hall. "Sorry, darlin'. I got caught in traffic or I'd have been here sooner." When she reached DJ, she wrapped her arms around her granddaughter and held her close.

"I can't do it, Gran. I can't go in there." The tears came, soaking Gran's shirt.

"Go ahead and cry it out." Gran stroked DJ's fuzz-covered head and dropped her own tears on the few remaining scabs. Though all DJ's hair had been singed off, the burns on her scalp had only been superficial. Her hands had taken most of the punishment. "Ah, darlin', we'll get through this. You go on in there and I'll wait right here, prayin' for God's mercy and strength. DJ, He promised He'd never give more than we can stand and that He's always right here with us."

"I . . . I know. . . . B-but it hurts so terrible," DJ sniffed between sobs. She took a shuddering breath and straightened in the chair. "Okay, Karen, let's g-go."

DJ bit off a whimper as they removed the bandages and air hit the burned tissue. One time she had looked and nearly thrown up at the sight of skinless, clawlike fingers that were red and crispy after the dense black tissue was scrubbed away. Now DJ kept her eyes closed. A groan made it past her clenched teeth. Sweat rolled down her face. The pain . . . the smell. Someone in another cubicle screamed. Tears poured down DJ's cheeks.

"Let it out, DJ. Screaming makes it easier." The therapist paused in the debridement and laid a hand on her shoulder. "Come on, kid, scream!"

DJ tried to bite her lip, but with the next pass of the brush she cried out. Another pass and the scream burst forth, beyond her control, from the deep place inside where she'd fought the battle. Her cries rang in her ears and rico-cheted down the corridors of her mind.

"There, now, kiddo. You did real good." Karen held her, murmuring in her ear and wiping the sweat away with a damp cloth. The cool cloth felt like heaven on DJ's skin.

It was over for another day. It had been a week since DJ woke from her coma, and it seemed as if she'd been count-ing the days from treatment to treatment and nothing else.

Gran met them in the hall, her own cheeks showing tear tracks and smeared mascara.

Together she and Karen got DJ back in bed and tucked in. Gran held a glass of ice water for DJ to sip. They had to keep forcing fluids into her, even with the IV still attached to her arm.

"You want a Popsicle or something?" Karen stroked across DJ's forehead and down her neck. "A back rub might help loosen you up some, too. That's an awful ordeal. I al-most cried with you."

"Really?"

"What do you think we nurses are, superhuman or something? Those guys down there in the therapy room, if they weren't absolutely convinced this was the best thing they could do for their patients, they'd never be able to get out of bed in the morning, let alone come in to work." As she talked, Karen bathed DJ's face and shoulders, rolled her on her side to rub in lotion to loosen the knots in her shoul-ders and neck, then adjusted the pillows. "There, now. Is that better?"

"Yes, thank you." DJ felt like purring. "And a banana Popsicle would be good."

Gran held it for her as she nibbled the cold treat, mop-ping her chin when DJ dribbled.

"I feel like a baby. I can't even hold my own Popsicle." DJ knew she sounded grumbly, but she also knew Gran wouldn't mind. Trying to keep a happy face was beyond her ability at times.

"You will be soon." Gran dropped the sticks in the wastebasket. "Looks to me like your boxing gloves are smaller."

DJ held up her hands. "Maybe." As the pain-killers kicked in, she could barely keep her eyes open. "I hate to sleep when you are here."

"Don't worry. I brought a book and sketch pad."

"How's GJ doing?" GJ stood for Grandpa Joe, DJ's nickname for her second grandfather. He had been married to Gran for about a year now. DJ barely remembered her first grandfather.

"Better. He just didn't dare bring his cold here. They wouldn't have let him in anyway. Got to keep you germ free."

"How's Major?" DJ's eyes drooped farther. Major was her first horse, whom she'd given to her cousin Shawna after Major was injured and could no longer jump.

"Fine. Shawna is working with him every day."

"And giving him all kinds of treats, right? He'll be spoiled to bits."

"She sent you a card—made it special for you." Gran dug in the big bag that accompanied her everywhere. She withdrew a big pink envelope and slit it open with one fingernail to show DJ the cartoon horse on the front. It wore bandages on its front legs and one eye.

DJ smiled. "She's getting good, huh?" Blinking her eyes helped keep them open.

Inside on the left of the card, Shawna had drawn a picture of Major with a balloon above his head that read, *When ya comin' home?* On the right another cartoon horse said,

Roses are red.
Ribbons are blue.
If you don't hurry home,
I'll come get you.

"Did you help her?" DJ tried to hide her second worst fear—that she would never draw again. How could she live without jumping or drawing? She'd helped Shawna not only with her riding, but drawing, as well. DJ and her best friend, Amy Yamamoto, had developed a greeting card line of DJ's drawings and Amy's photos—all horses. Sales were increasing; of their many money-earning schemes, it was the only one that really worked. Like her grandmother, DJ was already on her way to becoming an artist.

"Nope. Did it all herself." Gran held the horse drawings at arm's length and studied them. "Does real well for a ten-year-old." She smiled at DJ. "Not as good as you, of course, but she shows talent."

"Your mother has a box of cards for you at home. She'll bring them in tomorrow if her cold gets better. Seems the bug got the whole family down. So unseasonable, too."

DJ heard the last of Gran's words, but an answer refused to make it to her mouth. She woke sometime later to see Gran reading her book in the waning late-afternoon sunlight. Her sketch pad lay on the table beside her, her colored pencils back in their box. Gran had a new contract for another picture book that was still in the idea stage. As a well-known and award-winning illustrator, she always had plenty of work. DJ eyed the water glass. Her mouth felt like a herd of mustangs had galloped through it.

She cleared her throat. Sort of.

"Ah, you're awake." Gran put her things aside and crossed the room to bring DJ a drink.

DJ sucked on the straw as if she hadn't had a drink for a month. "Thanks. You read my mind."

Karen stuck her head in the doorway. "Hey, DJ, you ready for some visitors?"

"Who?"

"I'm not telling." Karen gave a horror-movie laugh and left.

DJ and Gran swapped questioning glances.

"Do I look all right?" DJ whispered. She had yet to see a mirror.

"Not even a zit." Gran laid a hand on DJ's shoulder. The sounds coming down the hall made DJ wish she could peek out the door.

2

"IS THIS THE ROOM of the famous DJ Randall?"

"Duh, I don't know, Chief. No sign on da door."

DJ could feel her eyebrows shoot up—if she still had eyebrows. A shiver tingled down her back. Who could it be?

"You think we should knock first?"

"Duh, I don't know, Chief. How do ya knock when da door is open?"

DJ could feel a giggle attack about to happen. She looked up to see Gran staring back at her, her eyes dancing. "What. . . ? Who?"

Gran shrugged.

"Duh, you wanna go first, Chief?"

"Of course. That's why they call me Chief." A loud clunking sound ended the arrival of four firemen in full fire-fighting gear—with red sponge noses. The first one wore a big sign that read *Chief*. One backed through the door because of the bright red box he and another carried.

"Duh, Chief, is dat DJ?" The one with the biggest nose leaned forward, pretending he couldn't see well.

"You mean that pretty lady standing by the bed or that cute chick who's giggling too hard to say hello?" The chief waggled his eyebrows.

DJ tried to stop laughing, but when the two men

waggled their eyebrows in tandem, she lost it. Gran's laughing didn't help.

"Duh, Chief, I tink dey likes us." He elbowed the man next to him and saluted DJ and Gran. "Dey call me Bozo. Dat's Chief, then Allen and . . ." He leaned closer to the fourth fireman. "What'd you say your name was? Okay. Yeah, Harvey, like da rabbit."

The other two firemen set their burden down where DJ could see it easily, and then all four men lined up at the foot of her bed, took off their helmets, clapped them over their hearts, and hummed "mi-mi-mi" in four-part harmony, then broke into "You Are My Sunshine."

"Duh, Chief, should we give her the present now?"

"Not yet, Bozo. Can't you remember anything?" The chief pretended to swat him with his helmet.

"Oh. Duh." Bozo shrugged and ducked.

The fireman named Allen stepped to the side of the bed. "Sure am glad to see you looking so well, DJ. The last time I saw you, things were mighty different."

"This is Fireman Allen White. He's the man who carried you out," the chief added to the introductions.

DJ fought the tears that not only threatened but trickled down her cheeks. "Th-thank you." She sniffed, and Gran leaned over with a tissue to wipe her nose and eyes.

"You're most welcome, little lady. We have a couple of things for you." White picked up a helmet that said *DJ* and set it on her head. "You are now an honorary member of the Morgan Hill Fire Fighters for saving all the lives of the horses with your quick thinking. You did the hard part. All we had to do was water down the barn."

"And save my granddaughter." Gran wiped her own eyes. "We can never thank you enough."

"Those kinds of things make our jobs worthwhile, ma'am." White, with his blond crew cut and toothpaste-ad smile in a tanned face, could have posed for a recruiting poster for firemen. He turned to his helper. "We have some other things here that just happened to show up at the fire-house. Thought you might enjoy them." He held up a video of the 1996 Olympics equestrian events and another of the movie *The Horse With the Flying Tail*, then pulled out a tod-dler-sized white bear with fur soft as a powder puff sitting in a black rubber bucket with brushes, combs, and curries. "We thought you probably lost yours in the fire."

DJ nodded. "I did. Thank you."

He took the bear out of the bucket and placed it on the pillow in the curve of DJ's arm. "The bear told us that you are quite an artist, so we thought maybe you could use these things, too. Not right now, of course, but soon." The box White opened held charcoal pencils, colored pencils, pastels, acrylic paints, brushes, drawing tablets in an as-sortment of sizes, and several stretched canvases. "Just an encouragement, of course."

DJ looked at her boxing-glove hands, then up to the men.

"Don't worry, DJ," White went on. "No matter what they look like now, your hands *will* hold a pencil again, and reins and brushes, too. This isn't the end of the road, but a big bump you gotta climb over or detour around. When you are jumping in the Olympics, we're going to be front and center, cheering you on like nobody's cheered before."

"I know you're going to have to work like you've never worked before, but the doc said you'd be all right again, and he never lies," the chief put in.

"Don't even stretch duh truth like that." Bozo elbowed the chief in the ribs. "Duh, dis guy here."

The chief snapped to attention. "I *always* tell the truth."

"How 'bout duh time . . ."

DJ giggled through her tears. "How can I ever thank you enough?"

"Just by keeping on keeping on. You call me when you

feel down. I've been there, and I know how bad it hurts."

"You do?"

White nodded. "Someday I'll come tell you my story. I've heard that sharing our stories is one way God brings good out of the hard things that happen to us. Like if I tell you my story and cheer you on, then when you are all better, you get to do the same for others. God is the original recycler. Nothing ever goes to waste."

Gran mopped DJ's eyes again.

"So you watch your movies and dream of flying over those jumps, okay?"

DJ nodded and sniffed. She raised her arms wide, and Allen White led the other firemen as they each gave her a hug.

"My name's really not Harvey, it's Kevin," the quiet fireman said. "And I know you can beat this."

"You go, girl. You're gonna do it," the chief whispered in her ear.

"I'll try."

"Nope, trying's not good enough. You just do it."

"Thanks. And thank you for all of this." DJ looked up to see three nurses, including Karen, standing in the doorway, drying their eyes.

"Hey, Fireman White, are you married?" DJ couldn't believe she said that.

"No, why?"

"'Cause Karen isn't, either, and she's really a super person."

Karen rolled her eyes and shot DJ an I'm-going-to-get-you-for-that look.

White strolled over to Karen. "What the princess wishes is my command. Will you go out with me, fair lady, or at least let me call you?"

Karen shook her head. "I . . ."

"You have to. It's DJ's wish."

"All right. You can call." Karen raised her hands in surrender.

"Good." DJ nodded her satisfaction. Allan White was one good-looking dude, and Karen looked good in a red face.

A beeper went off, and the chief unsnapped it from his lapel. He read the display, then said, "Sorry, DJ, but we gotta go."

"Thank you again for all of this, but mostly for coming." DJ sniffed again. "I'm not usually such a crybaby."

"That's okay. If you're a sissy, then there are five of us. See you." White winked and went out the door.

As they trooped down the hall, DJ heard, "Duh, Chief, can I push the elevator button?"

Gran and DJ swapped rolled-eye looks and shook their heads. "That Bozo."

"What a couple of clowns and a fine bunch of men. I wish Joe had been here. He'd have loved it." Joe had served on the San Francisco police force until his retirement. Major had been his horse for his last years on the mounted patrol and retired with Joe, who sold him to DJ.

"They sure were funny." DJ chuckled again and gave the bear a squeeze. "Feel how soft he is." But while she squeezed the bear with a smile on her face, she studied the drawing supplies. Would she ever be able to hold a pencil again, or the reins of her horse? She tried flexing her fingers, but the pain made her catch her breath.

"Okay, Darla Jean Randall, we have to talk." Karen tried to keep a fierce look on her face but failed by the time she reached the bed.

"My name is DJ."

"Nope, not now. Think of me as your mother. Darla Jean, what got into you?"

"He's cute, huh?"

"Better than cute, but how could you do that?"

DJ shrugged. "I don't know. It just slipped out."

Karen dug in her pocket and pulled out a business card. "Look at this. He gave me his card."

"Well, if he's as nice as he is good-looking, you two will make quite a pair." Gran lifted the helmet from the pillow behind DJ where she had set it earlier. "Honorary member, eh? What an honor."

"Wait until the Double Bs see this." At Karen's questioning look, DJ added, "The Double Bs are my twin brothers, Bobby and Billy. The only time you can tell them apart is when one is wearing a bandage or a bruise."

The bedside phone rang and Gran answered it. "It's Amy."

"I'll let you talk, since I'm sure my other patients are feeling neglected." Karen headed for the door.

"Bet the others don't introduce you to good-looking firemen." DJ giggled at the look Karen sent her, then nudged the phone into the hollow of her shoulder and ear.

"What was that all about?" Amy asked. When DJ was done telling the story, both girls were laughing. Gran periodically rolled her eyes and shook her head.

"Totally unbelievable."

"I know. How are things at the barns and school?"

"We miss you something awful."

When Gran hung the phone up sometime later, DJ closed her eyes. All kinds of good things were going on without her while she lay in a hospital bed, not even able to go to the bathroom by herself. She hugged the bear and let his soft fur soak up the tears. *What a crybaby you are. Come on, you're tougher than this*, the little voice in her head scolded.

"I hear you had company today," Dr. Niguri said when

he came in a while later. The clatter of dinner trays and the smell of something barbecued preceded him.

"She sure did." Gran pointed to the helmet.

"Firemen, eh? Looks like they brought the store."

DJ nodded. "And the bear."

Dr. Niguri studied the clipboard that held DJ's chart. "Looks to me like you're doing well. Any way I can help?"

"Let me go home?"

"Sorry. As much as I'd love to do that, you'll be here awhile."

"Awhile?" *Please, please give me a time when I can go home.*

"'Fraid so, DJ. We need to do some skin grafts and see how they take. Burns take a lot of care, and we want to make sure you can do everything again that you could before. So bear with us, okay?"

DJ nodded; the lump in her throat made answering too difficult. Days, weeks, what?

3

"I BROUGHT YOUR SCHOOL BOOKS," Mom said a week later.

DJ groaned and shook her head, trying to match her mother's smile but failing miserably. "How can I do school-work when I sleep all the time from the pain medication?" Lindy had been there only a few minutes and already DJ wished for Gran. Schoolwork was the last thing on DJ's mind.

Lindy Crowder eased her pregnant bulk down into the chair and sighed. "I know it will be hard, but maybe if you have something to concentrate on, the time will go faster. Besides, you've already missed two weeks of school—we can't let you get any further behind."

"I guess." DJ blinked and blinked again. If she could rub her eyes, that might get some clearness back into them. "At least I don't have algebra this year."

"You could take geometry, you know." The arch of her mother's eyebrows said she was teasing. DJ hated math like cats hated baths.

"You look so nice," DJ said. As usual, her mother's hair swung back into smooth sheets at the turn of her head. And though she wore a maternity sundress, she wore it with her normal flair, bright red-and-yellow dangly earrings, bracelets, and low espadrille shoes in the same yellow tone. Her face had rounded out a bit, but she had been careful about her weight and looked like she was carrying only a soccer ball under her dress.

"Mom, next to you, I feel creepy-cruddy."

"Darla Jean, what a thing to say. I'm fat as a hippo."

"Yeah, right." DJ didn't know much about pregnant women, but her mother surely didn't resemble any hippo she'd ever seen.

"Your hair is coming back. Every time I see you it's longer."

"You mean now I look like I have a crew cut instead of a shave?"

"Something like that—almost. I could bring you a perky bow and tape it to the top, like I did when you were a baby."

"Thanks, but no thanks. At least it doesn't itch so much." DJ eyed the stack of books on her bedside table. "How am I supposed to read those when I can't even turn the pages?"

"Joni Eareckson Tada turns her pages with a pencil or something held in her mouth. We can prop the book on this." Lindy swung the bed table over and opened the tray, setting the book in place. The book snapped closed. "Hmm. There's gotta be a way around this." She handed DJ an unsharpened pencil. "You use the eraser end to turn the pages."

"Have you tried this?"

"No, but maybe I should have. Guess I'll ask the nurses if they have any suggestions. In the meantime, when any of us come to visit, we can take turns reading to you. See, here in the notebook is your list of assignments according to class."

"How are the Bs?"

"Good. They think first grade is a lark. Not being able to tell them apart is driving their teacher nuts. You want a drink?"

"Yes, please, and a Popsicle."

Lindy pushed herself up by using the arms of the chair. "Whew! How come everything seems so far down?" She started for the door, then turned. "But after that we do history."

"How about lit instead?"

"Whatever."

But before she returned, DJ had dozed off again. She woke to see her mother tapping away at her laptop computer, the Popsicle melted in a dish on the bed table.

"Sorry." Her croak sounded more like a toad than a girl.

"No problem. Mother warned me how often this happens. At least when you're sleeping you don't hurt, and that's most important." Lindy held the glass of ice water for DJ to drink from the straw and motioned to the yellow Popsicle liquid. "I could spoon that for you."

" 'Kay. But I gotta go to the bathroom first. Call the nurse." She nodded to the push buttons on the bed rail.

"Can't I help you?"

"I guess, but . . ."

"Darla Jean, I'm your mother. And just because I'm pregnant doesn't mean I'm a weakling, you know."

"Sorry." DJ did her sideways-moving crab imitation to the edge of the bed and swung her feet over the side while at the same time rolling up into a full sitting position.

"Hey, you're getting pretty good at that. Now, what do you want me to do?"

"Hang on to me so that I don't slip when I stand, and then we walk together. I don't get dizzy so often now, but sometimes the room turns into a carousel." By the time they got DJ back into bed, both of them were giggling over Lindy's belly being in the way.

"Hey, did we tell you that we think this muffin in here is probably a girl?" Lindy patted her bulge with one hand and held DJ's water glass with the other. "She finally turned right so the sonogram could tell. How about helping me with names for your new sister?"

"Wow. That is totally awesome."

"I even have pictures." Lindy whipped out a folder with a shadowy form in a black-and-white picture. "See, there's her head, hands, and feet. Isn't she beautiful?"

DJ raised what eyebrows she had grown back. "Beautiful? Mo-ther!"

"Well, I guess beauty is in the eye of the beholder. But I got to watch her moving around, and, DJ, she even put her thumb in her mouth. Can you believe that?" Lindy's eyes glimmered through the sheen of tears. "I've been thinking of calling her Grace because she is such a wonderful gift."

"Grace." DJ tried it out. "Kinda old-fashioned, isn't it?"

"I know. Maybe that could be her middle name. So help me think of something. Robert wants to call her Amelia, after his mother."

"Then she'd be Amelia Grace." DJ shook her head. "Not quite right." But much as she tried, no good ideas came. In fact, one of the scary things was that her mind didn't seem to be working. All DJ wanted to do was sleep.

"A sister. I'm going to have a baby sister." Seeing the picture and thinking about names made this baby, which had seemed so far off, a pretty-soon reality.

"Something to think about, isn't it?" Lindy flinched. "Oof, she's going to be a soccer star for sure." She laid her hand on the side where even DJ could see the baby kick, moving her mother's sundress.

"Wow! Doesn't that hurt?"

"Let me tell you." Lindy sucked in a deep breath and let it all out. "And to think I have more than three months to go."

DJ shifted in the bed, rolling over so she could see her mother better. "Have the Bs been riding?"

"Every day. They're working on a surprise for you, but I promised I wouldn't tell."

"Mother, that's mean."

"Just another good reason to get you out of here as soon as possible. We all miss you so terribly. Home just isn't the same without you there." Lindy blinked several times. "I find Queenie up in your room every once in a while, lying there by your bed waiting for you."

DJ could feel tears at the back of her eyes. They'd found Queenie, a black-and-white mixed breed, at the Humane Society, and she had taken over as if she'd lived with them all her life.

"So no more procrastinating. You want U.S. history or lit? According to the schedule your teacher sent, you have a book report due in two weeks. I asked her if you could use an audio tape instead, and she agreed, so you need to choose a book. Here's the list of audios available. It has to be one of the classics."

"Yuck."

"I thought you might like *Tom Sawyer*. I remember loving that book when I was your age."

DJ shrugged. "I guess. Couldn't I watch the movie instead?"

"Book report equals reading . . . or at least listening. If that's the one you'd like, I'll bring it and a tape recorder with me day after tomorrow."

DJ thought a moment. *How will I keep track of the story? I can hardly keep track of my own name.* "How will I turn the thing on and off?"

"Your handy-dandy mouth tool." Lindy waved the pencil, then looked at it. "Hmm, needs to be something longer than that. I'll let Robert devise us something." She laid a hand on her daughter's shoulder. "We can make it work, Deej. I know it's really hard for you, but we'll all help. Bobby said he had to learn to read real quick so he could help you with your homework. And Billy said he'd learn faster. You won't be here in the hospital forever."

"Even though it seems like it, huh?"

"Even though."

The evening nurse squeaked her way into the room and up to the side of the bed. "How about taking a walk down the hall, kiddo? Stretch those legs a bit."

DJ glanced up at the IV bag. "With that?"

"Sure. I'll push it for you."

"Really?" DJ twitched her nose. The nose prongs for oxygen had begun to seem like part of her body. The doctor said she needed the oxygen because her lungs were still healing from all the smoke damage.

"But you won't be lifting weights or running any races, promise?" The nurse, a middle-aged black woman, looked over her half glasses, trying to look stern. "From what I hear about you, you'd bring your horse right in here, too."

"Oh, could we?"

Thela, as she'd introduced herself, rolled her eyes and began disconnecting the oxygen line. "What a girl." Together, Thela and DJ maneuvered into the hallway with the IV stand, Lindy close behind.

Though DJ had been managing the trek to the bathroom, which was right across the room, by the time she reached the corner of the hall and looked back, her room looked a mile away and her legs and chest were doing a wobbly dance.

"C-can I sit down?"

"Of course, child. Should never have brought you this far." Thela snagged a wheelchair that sat along the wall and set the brakes. "Now, I'm not going to take you back in this, but . . ."

DJ sat down quickly and closed her eyes. The hall, too, had taken to dancing, up and down and in circles.

"Let me rephrase that." Thela flipped the footrests into

position. "Since you are riding back in the wheelchair, you can keep your eyes closed. Do you need to put your head down? You're not going to faint or throw up, are you?"

"No." The word came out in a whisper. At least she wouldn't if she kept her eyes closed—she hoped. How embarrassing. Her mother's cool hand felt good on the back of her neck.

As soon as she was tucked back in bed and hooked up again, DJ made her lips smile whether they wanted to or not. "Thanks for the ride."

"You're welcome, sweet thing. We sure do have to get you built back up."

"So I can go home."

"Right. Let me listen here." Thela applied the stethoscope to DJ's chest. "Take a deep breath."

DJ did as asked and a cough exploded. When she could quit hacking, she lay back, limp as Herndon's used leg wrappings.

Thela rubbed her ear. "Serves me right. I asked for that."

DJ nodded to the water pitcher. "Mom, could I have a drink, please?"

"Sure." Lindy filled the plastic glass. Her eyes shot question marks at the nurse, who studied her patient.

"Need some pain meds?"

DJ nodded. Now not only did her hands hurt, but her chest did again, too. And the cough had started a headache. In fact, if she thought about it, which she tried not to do, she hurt about everywhere a person could hurt.

Not long after Thela injected the medication into the IV, DJ began to feel like she was floating again, as if she would bounce off the ceiling pretty soon.

"Better?"

DJ nodded and turned her head to look at her mother. "You better get going."

"No hurry." Lindy held the glass again so DJ could drink.

"I'm beginning to think we ought to get you a tube so you can suck water at your own speed." Her mother's voice came from a long distance away.

"Umm . . ."

"I love you, Darla Jean Randall."

"Me too. Night, Mom."

"Oh, one more thing. There might be a surprise for you tomorrow."

"Really?" DJ's eyes popped open. "What?"

"Ah, I won't tell." Lindy kissed her on the cheek.

"Oh, my goodness." Karen turned from looking out the window. "DJ, you won't believe this."

"Okay, what's up?" DJ had finished her breakfast with many interruptions. Karen would stop feeding her to keep glancing out the window.

"Nothing, nothing at all." But the glint in her eyes said something different.

"What's going on?"

4

"WHAT IS IT?" DJ insisted.

Karen crossed back from the window to DJ's bed. "Come on, girl. You gotta see this." She lowered the bed rail and grasped DJ's upper arm to help her sit up and swing her legs over the edge. "Let me get your IV pole and you'll be truckin'."

The grin on her face promised something special.

"Can't you tell me what it is?" DJ craned her neck, hoping to see over the windowsill. Nada.

"*Can't* is the right word." With all the tubing hooked over the pole's supports, Karen brought the clanking stand around the end of the bed and braced DJ with her other arm so she wouldn't slip. "Shoulda just lowered the bed."

"Good thing I've got long legs, huh?" DJ felt for her slippers and slid her feet into them. How come even the distance to the window seemed like such a hike? How would she ever get back in shape after all this lying around? She blinked as the room shifted. Although the doctor told her that was normal for someone with a head injury and on so much pain medication, shifting walls were still scary. Sometimes DJ woke up thinking she might be this way for the rest of her life. At least at this time of the morning she was less woozy than later in the day.

She slammed the door in her mind against the thought of *later in the day*. The treatments came on like a runaway horse whether she tried not to think of them or not.

"You ready?" Karen's voice had gone from joyful to gentle.

"Yeah. Did I zone out again?"

"Only a little. Not to worry." With Karen pushing the pole, they shuffle-clanked their way to the window.

DJ looked down into the hospital parking lot. The first thing she saw was a familiar horse trailer attached to her grandfather's pickup. She looked straight down, closer to the building. A bunch of grinning faces topped a long sign held up by lots of willing hands. The sign read *We miss you, DJ. Get well fast!* The hands belonged to all her friends from Briones Riding Academy, where DJ stabled her horse and taught younger kids to ride. Amy stood front and center, jumping up and down and waving both arms. Major, DJ's first horse and dear friend, pricked his ears and, when her cousin Shawna tapped his knee, bowed.

"Circus tricks. She's teaching him circus tricks. How funny."

"Who?"

"Major. He's such a sweetie."

"You want the window open?"

"Yes, please."

DJ leaned close to the screen and whistled her special high-low greeting for Major. He looked around, searching for her. She whistled again, and he raised his head, looked right at her, and nickered, nodding as if to say, "Get on down here. What are you doing way up there?"

Shawna, now Major's owner, waved and yelled, "Can you come out to play?"

The others hollered their greetings.

Other nurses and medical people gathered in DJ's room

to cheer, too, and many from the first floor filled the front walk and clapped along.

Fighting tears, DJ swallowed, looked upward, did everything she knew to stem the flow, but nothing helped. Her friends had given up their Saturday to come all this way to see her. After all, the UC San Francisco hospital wasn't just around the corner from their homes in Pleasant Hill.

"So do you want to go down there?" Karen touched DJ's shoulder to get her attention.

"Can I?"

"Sure. I'll grab us a wheelchair. You have to promise not to ride the horse or even get too close, but . . ." Karen glanced at the nursing supervisor, who nodded. "After all, they came all this way."

"Don't go away," DJ called through the window. "I'm coming down." She glanced down at her hospital gown and up at Karen. "In this?"

Karen shrugged. "I guess we'll wrap a sheet around you. Nothing goes over those boxing gloves of yours."

Within minutes DJ and her entourage blew out the front doors and up the sidewalk to where her friends waited.

"Now, here are the rules." Karen held up her hand like a traffic cop. "If you have a cold, stay back, no one can touch her, and she can't go riding."

The last comment made everyone laugh.

"How did the rest of the show go?" DJ looked from Tony Andrada to Hilary Jones, who'd both been at the show at Rancho de Equus.

"I won Juniors."

"And I did Intermediates."

"And Bunny got third in her class."

"We cleaned up." The answers all overlapped and ran together.

"We sure miss you teaching our class," her three girl students added.

"You can teach even if your hands are bandaged. You know, when you get home," Angie said. "We need you."

"Thanks."

"Oh, and Bridget said to tell you she'll come by in the next few days. She has something she wants to talk over with you." Tony hunkered down beside DJ's wheelchair. "It would be cool if you could come to the classic at the end of this month and cheer us on."

DJ looked up at Karen, who shrugged. "Once we get you out of here, everything will depend on how well you feel."

"Does it still hurt bad?" Shawna asked.

DJ nodded and rolled her eyes. "Like nothing I can describe."

"Can I bring Major closer?" Shawna asked Karen. "He wants to show her something."

"I guess, if he won't be spooked by the pole and chair and stuff."

"Major?" The look of shock on Shawna's face matched DJ's.

"He's a retired police horse. Took a bullet in the shoulder and kept on working. Nothing scares him." DJ rested her elbows on the arms of the chair. Why did just sitting in a chair and chatting with her friends make her tired?

Shawna led the big bay through the group and up to the chair. Major studied DJ as if trying to figure out what had happened to her, then reached forward and nuzzled her cheek, wuffling in her ear. DJ leaned her cheek against his nose and ignored the tears that streamed down her cheeks.

"Oh, Major, you smell so good."

He sniffed the top of her head and raised his nose, rolling his upper lip back.

"Guess I don't, huh? Remind you of the hospital you were in?" DJ laughed through her tears.

"He sure doesn't think you smell good." Karen laughed with the rest. The minutes flew by like seconds as they all caught DJ up on the latest at Briones and the beginning of school.

Finally Karen glanced at her watch. "Sorry, kids, but DJ has a date with therapy in a few minutes, and I better make sure there's not a horsehair on her. Come say your good-byes."

After all the others filed by, some leaving cards in her lap, Joe squatted down in front of her chair, his knees creaking loud enough to make the others laugh again.

"I'll be up later, now that I'm well enough to pass inspection. You do what they tell you, okay? We need you home yesterday."

DJ wanted to throw her arms around his neck, to bolt from the wheelchair and leave IV poles and hospital gowns and the coming torture far behind. "Thanks for coming."

"We're all praying for you." He glanced around at the group, who all nodded. "And lots of others, too. God can handle anything, even burn therapy."

But, GJ, it hurts so bad. I can't stand it. Instead of saying the words, DJ just nodded.

"Okay, DJ, we're outta here. Wave to your admirers," Karen instructed.

"See you all. Thanks for coming. Bye, Major."

Shawna tapped his knee, and Major stretched one leg in front of him, put his nose on his knee, and bowed.

"I can't believe this. Major, the horse of many lives." DJ waved again. She sat straight until Karen wheeled her through the doors, then slumped in her chair. "I feel like I've run a marathon, and I haven't even been out of this stupid chair."

"Hey, don't call this elegant mode of transportation stupid. It might quit, and then where would you be?" But Karen patted DJ's shoulder as they waited for the elevator. "You'll make it, DJ. And I know how you dread the hours ahead. Everyone does."

"It isn't just the treatment. I hate what the drugs do to my mind. All I want to do is sleep."

"I know. But the more we can control the pain for you, the faster your body will heal. It takes a tremendous amount of energy for your body to produce all the new cells to remake your hands, fight off any infection, and even grow new hair—which, by the way, cute as yours is coming in, you might start a new style."

"So I'm not just a wuss?" DJ stared down at her bandaged hands, her words barely a whisper.

"Oh, DJ, has that been bothering you?" Karen squatted and put a hand on DJ's arm. "I have seen tough men—men who went to war, even—faint from the pain of the burn treatments. I've heard them screaming like they might never quit. One woman patient said she'd rather have ten kids by natural childbirth than ever go through anything like that again—and I tell you, she was tough. But she told me it's easier if you scream. And I believe that screaming lets the tension out so the body can concentrate on healing, not on keeping the hurt inside."

"Really?" A tear slipped down DJ's cheek. "I hate crying all the time."

"I know. But tears help with the healing, too. There are special chemicals released in tears that are better on your cheeks than inside." She stroked DJ's fuzzy hair.

"Now you sound like Gran."

"Well, that grandmother of yours is one dynamite lady. I feel privileged to get to know her."

"Me too." DJ sniffed. "You got a Kleenex?"

"I sure do." Karen dug in her smock pocket and used the tissue she found there to wipe DJ's eyes and nose. "Now, we have fifteen minutes or so until we head to the little room of horrors. You want to stay in the chair or opt for the bed?"

"Bed, please." DJ sniffed again. "Thanks, Karen. You've helped me a lot."

They had just gotten her back into bed when Gran breezed into the room. "Whew, I made it in time today." She set her bag down on the chair and leaned over to give DJ a hug. "So they all got here all right?"

"Sure did. Half the hospital went out to watch." Karen finished checking all the equipment. "You two visit, and I'll be back when they call for us."

"So how was it? I planned to drive in the caravan, but my agent called right then and I needed to talk with her."

"Did you know that Shawna has been teaching Major tricks?"

"Of course, darlin'. Joe's been helping her. Those two get to laughin', and Major looks at them like they lost their horse cookies. Funniest thing you ever saw."

"How are the boys doing with General?" DJ looked at Gran from the side of her eyes. "They're not teaching *him* tricks, too, are they?"

"Not that I know of, but I think he already knew a few. You know, I think Shawna has a real gift for training animals. She's got Queenie—whoops." Gran clamped her hand over her mouth. "Promise me you won't tell anyone that I almost let that slip, please?"

"I won't tell if you let it slip a bit more so I know what's going on."

"No can do. I'd lose my grandmother status."

"G-r-a-n."

"Nope, I promised." She crossed her heart with one finger. "I even crossed my heart. You wouldn't want me to break a promise, would you? Besides, it gives you something to look forward to." Gran dug in her voluminous bag. "The boys sent you . . . Ah, here it is." She pulled out an envelope with horses stamped all over it. "They got a bit carried away, but they were having fun." She laid the envelope on the white bedspread and began digging again. "Your mother sent something, too."

"More homework?"

"No, pages from her book. I said I'd read them to you so you could let her know what you think."

"She brought homework yesterday." DJ nodded toward the pile of books on her nightstand. "She's going to rig up something so I can turn the pages with my teeth." DJ rolled her eyes and shook her head.

"Sounds like a good idea to me. Maybe we should employ readers. Once you get home, there'll be plenty of people willing to help."

"Sorry to interrupt, ladies," Karen said as she came into the room. "They're ready for us."

DJ felt her whole body tense up as if some giant had grabbed her head and feet and wrung her like a dishcloth. *God, please help me. I can feel a scream coming already.* "I don't want to go."

5

"IS IT OVER?"

"Yes, darlin'. You fainted. Best thing that could have happened, far as I'm concerned."

"I fainted?" DJ could feel her brow wrinkling. "How long ago?"

"Oh, they brought you back here and you woke a bit, but the pain-killers put you to sleep again without you becoming much aware." Gran glanced up from her sketch pad. "It's evening now. You feel like eating?"

"Not really." DJ looked at her hands. The bandages were a bit smaller, but not much. "I remember someone screaming. Was it me?"

"Oh, you and a couple others. As Karen says, screaming is better than holding it in."

"Hey, if I could faint every time . . . It wasn't so bad." DJ could feel the weights pulling down her eyelids again. "Will you be here when I wake up again?"

"If not me, maybe Joe or Robert. He's feeling left out."

"Joe?"

"No, Robert. He and the boys miss you terribly."

DJ tried to answer, but the tide of sleep swept her out.

"Hey, Deej, welcome back." Robert set his book aside and leaned on the raised rails of DJ's bed. "Had to come see for myself that you are getting better. Not that I don't trust the others, but . . ."

"Hi, Dad."

Robert blinked his appreciation of her use of "Dad" and reached out to run the knuckle of his right forefinger down her cheek, the tenderness of the gesture bringing a smile to DJ's pale face. "You have no idea how much it means to me to hear you call me that."

"I'm pretty lucky, you know. Two cool dads." DJ tried to clear the frog out of her throat and smiled her thanks when Robert held the glass for her.

"You want more than water?"

DJ thought a moment. Getting her mind to leave the muzziness of la-la land and come back to work took some doing. "I think I'm hungry. And maybe some Gatorade or something would taste good."

"Great. I'll go tell the nurse. They put your dinner in the fridge to save for when you woke up." He rose and stood looking down at DJ. "I am mighty glad you're still with us. I mean, I know heaven is a wonderful place, but this one would be a lot less happy if you were gone."

"Thanks." DJ's eyes burned and her nose started to run. "Now you have to wipe my nose, please."

Robert pulled out two tissues. "Mine too." He held the tissue to her nose. "Now blow. See? I can do this. I just got the twins to blow their own noses, and now I can help you. Keeps me in practice for the baby."

"How's Mom?"

"How about we talk when I get back?" He tapped the end of her nose and headed for the door.

"Hi, sugar, welcome back to the land of the livin'." Thela wore a smile that crinkled her black eyes nearly shut. "You sure are our celebrity after today." She leaned closer. "You didn't really get kissed by a horse, did you?"

"Not just any horse, but Major, the sweetest horse to gallop this earth." DJ dropped her voice to a conspiratorial whisper. "But Karen made sure all the horsehairs were brushed away before any doctors saw them."

"That Karen's one smart girl. I'm surprised they didn't bring the horse clear up here."

"Really? Would they?"

"Well, there've been dogs, cats, rabbits, a boa once. . . ." Thela squinted her eyes. "Oh yeah, monkeys, a pot-bellied pig, ferrets—one got loose, and if that wasn't a circus in itself—and miniature horses. You know, nothing helps sick folks get better faster than a warm, furry critter to hug on. Not all the doctors agree with that, but we nurses know the real skinny."

"Wow, I never thought hospitals did such things." DJ thought of Queenie. "Our dog would be good for something like that. She's so smart and well behaved."

"Mostly we do things like that up on the oncology ward where kids have to be here a long time. Clowns and music groups come to visit. Even movie stars and sports heroes sometimes. Lots of people give their time to help patients get well again."

"Like the firemen who came to see me."

"True, but they came because they had a vested interest in you, like the one who saved your life." Thela stepped back. "I think your dinner must be warm by now. You want me to help you?"

"No, I will," Robert answered before DJ could.

"Thela, this is my dad Robert Crowder."

"Oh, we've met." The nurse got a puzzled look and shook her head. "But the voice doesn't match. A man who said he was your dad called here a while ago when you were still sleeping to inquire about how you were doin', and his voice was different."

"Oh, that's my other dad, Brad Atwood."

"Yeah, that's the name."

"And Joe Crowder is my grandfather. You've probably heard from him, too. He brought Major and some of the Briones kids over this morning."

Thela shook her head again. "Girl, you sure got lots of good-lookin' men in your life. Nice too."

You don't know the half of it. Two years ago I didn't have any men in my life—and had no idea how much I was missing. "You haven't met my twin brothers yet, either. Six-year-old dynamos, Bobby and Billy. I sure miss them."

"They've been missing you, too," Robert said. "In fact, I got an extra kiss on each cheek to pass along to you from them."

"I'd say, young lady, God's been blessin' your socks off." Thela headed for the door. "Guess I better go take care of my other patients."

"You're right, Thela. I haven't worn socks for over two weeks now." DJ giggled at the snort of laughter she heard from the hall.

"Ah, daughter, I sure am glad you can still joke." Robert cut the chicken breast and held a bite up to DJ's mouth. "Now, open wide and the little train will chug right in."

DJ looked from the fork to Robert's laughing blue eyes, so like those of the twins. She nearly choked on the laughter that grabbed her throat. "A . . . a train?" The laughter made her cough. "Water, I need water."

Robert dropped the fork on her lap and, reaching for the water glass, hit the open milk carton, which spilled over the edge of the tray and dripped on DJ's legs.

"Good grief! I've lost my touch."

As soon as DJ's throat cleared, she let out a hoot that could be heard all the way to the nurses' station, even if the intercom hadn't been on. Several pairs of squeaky shoes beat a path to the doorway. Thela rushed into the room while the others blocked the door.

"What in the world?" Hands on her hips, dark brown arms akimbo, Thela shook her head, then began mopping up the mess, her hands bumping into Robert's as he tried to help. "My land, I'll bet those boys of yours don't need any help at the table, not if they have any sense." She pushed his hands away. "You sit!" She pointed at the chair, and Robert obeyed.

DJ laughed so hard, tears streaked down her face.

Robert gave her a kicked-puppy look that made both DJ and Thela laugh even harder. The other nurses could be heard giggling down the hall.

"Well, I'm happy to be the object of everyone's amusement." Robert sat back and locked his arms over his chest. "See if I try to help *you* eat again."

"See if we let you." Thela wiped DJ's eyes and cheeks, then gave her a bite of baked potato. "Best thing that could happen is to get you laughin' like this, but he sure gives me a mess to clean up, that man." She sent him what was meant to be a withering look, but the way her eyes danced made DJ laugh again.

Robert attempted a wounded look. "I didn't do it on purpose."

"That sounds like one of the Bs." DJ nodded to the milk carton to indicate she wanted a drink. "If there is any left, that is."

"I can always get you another." Thela shook the container. "After this."

When DJ refused any more food, and the nurse took the tray out, Robert pointed toward the stack of school books. "Which shall we start with?"

"History." DJ sighed. "If I can stay awake long enough."

"You want me to run you up and down the hall?"

"No, I want you to take me home."

"Ah, if only I could, it would be the greatest honor in the

world. But in the meantime, here we go." Robert pulled out the history book and studied the sheet of assignments tucked in the front. "You should be through chapter two by now."

"But Mom just brought them yesterday."

Robert gave her a beats-me shrug and flipped the pages.

DJ tried to concentrate on what he was saying, but her eyes insisted that remaining open was beyond their strength.

"Are you listening?"

"Sure."

"So what did I just read?"

"About Eric the Red finding the coast of Greenland."

"Oh." He kept on reading.

"No! No!" DJ thrashed from side to side. "No!" She banged her hand against the bed rails, screaming from the pain.

"DJ, what is it? What's wrong?" A nurse flew through the door and up to the bed.

"I . . . I think I had a nightmare." DJ could hardly draw a breath. Her jaw ached. Her hand kept on screaming with pain.

"Easy, now. Breathe slowly. Here, how about a drink?" The lights had been dimmed for the night, leaving shadows in the corners of the room. The balloons bobbed in the draft, catching DJ's attention. One glinted as it bobbed, as if alive and coming after her.

She stifled a groan. *All this because of a bad dream? Get a grip, girl.* The voice in her head mocked the sweat beading on her upper lip. "When did my dad go home?"

"Quite some time ago. It's nearly 1:00 A.M." The nurse mopped DJ's face with a warm washcloth. "You better now?

Sure would hate to take your blood pressure and have it through the ceiling."

DJ leaned back against her pillows. "Yes, thank you. I dreamed someone had a pillow over my face and wouldn't let up. I couldn't breathe." She sucked on the straw like she might never drink again.

"Not surprising since your lungs were damaged by the smoke."

"But it was so real."

"I know." The nurse grasped DJ's wrist to check her pulse. "Some of the meds you're on could induce that kind of thing, too. Sorry I couldn't get here sooner."

DJ stared up at the ceiling. "Sorry to be such a bother." She waited as the nurse applied the blood pressure cuff. When that was done, she asked, "You think we could get me to the bathroom before you leave again?"

"Sure, unless you want to use a bedpan."

"Ugh." DJ shuddered. "I'll walk."

The next morning Dr. Niguri entered the room just as DJ finished her breakfast. He finished jotting something on the clipboard, then studied her over the top of his glasses.

"Looks like you had a rather restless night."

"I guess."

"And here I hoped you would be all rested and cheerful to hear some good news."

"I'm rested. I'm cheerful." DJ opened her eyes and smiled as wide as she could. A yawn caught her, forcing her mouth wide open.

"Ah, I see you still have your tonsils."

"Sorry."

"I can tell you are too sleepy. I'll come back later." He spun on his heel and headed for the door.

"Wait. Please? Don't go."

6

DR. NIGURI STOPPED AT THE DOOR. "How would you like to go home in a week or two?"

"How about tomorrow?" DJ wished she could reach out and grab the words back. Whatever had gotten into her?

Dr. Niguri shook his head, smiling at the same time. "I can tell you are feeling better when you try to bargain. I'd love to send you home tomorrow, today even, but I can't take a chance on that. I've set you up for skin grafts tomorrow, and if they take like I think they will, we'll be seeing you as an outpatient. Or perhaps we can shift your care over to a hospital nearer to your home for rehab therapy. How does all that sound to you?"

"Like good news." DJ studied her bandaged hands. "How long until I can use my hands?"

"I can't give you a good answer on that. I know 'it all depends' sounds lame, but there are so many variables yet."

Will I be able to ride again? Even the thought made DJ's gut clench. *Come on, ask. Don't be such a chicken.* "But . . . but . . ." She sucked in a deep breath that started her coughing. He waited patiently until she caught her breath and could speak again. "Will . . . will I be able to . . ." She stopped, unable to force the words past the lump swelling in her throat.

Dr. Niguri sat down on the edge of the bed. "To ride again?"

DJ nodded, unable to look him in the face. *What if he says no? God, I can't stand the thought of never riding again.*

"I don't see why not. It will take time and a lot of hard work to regain your small-muscle control, but I believe it will come back. Damaged nerves grow back, as does muscle. You'll never have your original fingerprints, and there may be more surgeries ahead, but I believe with lots of work, this will happen. The most important thing you can do is keep from getting discouraged."

"Sometimes I'm so scared," the whispered words finally came out.

"Perfectly normal. Who wouldn't be? The pain of burns is like no other. Think how people even groan about a sunburn. Burns are painful beyond words, as I know you've figured out. But we can do amazing things these days to restore the burned area to its former beauty and usefulness. You've just got to be patient."

"It's so hard."

"I know. Patience has never been my main strength, either." He leaned back and crossed one ankle over the other knee. "Any other questions?"

"My mom brought in my homework. How can I do that when I keep falling asleep?"

"In bits and pieces. Concentration is difficult when you are still on so much pain medication, but we have to control the pain as much as possible so your body can put its energy into healing. Down the road we can give you some other things that won't mess with your mind so much."

DJ made a face. "Karen talked with you, huh?"

"Yep. We might have some volunteers here who could read to you. I'll get the nurses to check on that. If this were to be a long-term disability, we could get you set up with a talking computer if someone scanned the pages of your textbooks into it."

He got to his feet. "I know this gives you a lot to think about, so I'll get these orders written." He waved the clipboard at her. "Just go easy on the horse kisses, okay?" He winked, patted her foot, and left the room.

"Home . . . I get to go home." DJ closed her eyes and pictured her room with all her art supplies and private bath with the Jacuzzi tub. Surely they could put a talking program on her own computer. The boys and Queenie would go crazy when she got there. She could probably get a speaker phone, too. She opened her eyes and looked at her hands. Would she be able to draw again? Not *if* but *when*. "I have to quit thinking about *if*. Bridget would have my head if she heard me talking about *if*."

"Talking to yourself, huh?" Karen came into the room to check on the beeping machines. "Hey, I got news for you."

"What?"

"Guess who I'm going out with tonight?"

"Allen White?"

"Cool, huh?"

"Really cool. Where you going?"

"Dinner and a movie." Karen reopened a valve on the IV and checked around the needle in DJ's arm. "Lookin' good, kid. You have strong veins and good nurses."

"I feel like a pincushion. They come for blood, more blood, then give me a shot for this, then another shot for that."

"I know. Sorry. I'll see if I can find a needle to stick you with now so you don't get too comfortable."

"Don't bother. But a Popsicle would be good, or ice cream."

"Coming right up. I'll find someone to feed it to you, too."

"Never mind, that's what I'm here for." Gran strolled into the room, followed by GJ.

"We're here."

"Karen, this is my grandpa. I call him GJ for Grandpa Joe."

"I met him yesterday, remember? He brought the horse. And thanks to you and all your helpful friends yesterday, they're calling me the horse lady. And I'm not even the one who got kissed."

"Karen's going on a date with Allen White, the fireman who saved my life." Funny how it was getting easier and easier to say that. In fact, since DJ's throat was so much better, talking about anything was easier now.

"Well, isn't that a fine idea?" Gran set down her satchel and leaned over to kiss DJ. "I hear Major didn't think you smelled too good."

"I know. He did the rolled-back-lips thing. So funny." DJ lifted a hand to what would have been her hair. "Maybe he didn't like my new hairstyle. I shoulda worn my fireman's hat."

Between Gran and Joe taking turns reading to her and poking her to stay awake, the morning passed quickly. Treatment time arrived before DJ had time to work up a good dread.

"You'll still be here when I get back?"

"Better than that. We'll go with you as far as they let us."

Joe kept them laughing down the halls as he told about the boys and Shawna teaching the horses tricks and how Queenie learned one from watching Shawna and Major.

"We'll sit right out here prayin' for you, darlin'. So don't you fret."

DJ blinked away the tears that even the sight of the door to the treatment room brought. "Let's get it over with." *Please, God, let me faint again.*

When DJ got back to her room, already groggy from the pain meds, the phone rang. Karen answered it. "Just a minute, okay? Let me get her comfortable and then she'd love to chat."

"Who?" DJ mouthed.

Karen nodded and smiled, all the while settling DJ back in bed, adjusting the nose prongs for oxygen, and tucking the phone between DJ's ear and shoulder.

"Hi, DJ, did you think we'd forgotten you?" Brad Atwood, her biological father, sounded as if he were in the room.

"Hi, Dad. I haven't had much time to think, if you want to know the truth."

"They say you are doing well."

"I guess. How are Jackie and Stormy and Herndon?"

"All missing you, like me." His voice choked. "I'm still having a hard time believing all this happened." He cleared his throat again. "You up for more visitors?"

"Always. Did you hear who came to see me?" She told him about Major and the Briones bunch and then the firemen.

"Red noses, huh? And Major doesn't think you smell nice. DJ, leave it to you. I bet that turned some of the hospital staff right upside down."

"I guess. I'll ask Karen, my nurse." DJ fought to keep her eyes open. "Dad, if you come, come in the evening when I am more awake. This pain stuff makes me so sleepy." A yawn caught her by surprise. "Give Stormy and Herndon each a horse cookie for me, okay?" Another yawn.

"Should I give Jackie one, too?"

"D-a-d."

When she hung up, DJ let her eyes shut.

"He sounds mighty nice, like the rest of your family."

52

"He is. Stormy is my Arab filly. I helped get her eating after . . ." She couldn't find words to finish the sentence.

"So you're going out with Allen White?" DJ nodded and grinned at the same time. It was several hours since the treatment, and DJ had returned to the world of the awake.

Karen sucked in a deep breath. "I guess. He's called twice. Seems like a really nice guy."

"Cute too." DJ giggled. "Your face is all red."

"Oh, I got something for you." Karen dumped several envelopes on the bed. "Mail came. You want me to open them for you?"

"Please."

"Ah, look at this one." Karen held up a hand-painted horse's head with a big tear coming from its eye. When she opened the card, DJ read, *I'm not very good with horses yet, but then, you haven't given me much instruction. Get well soon so we can go drawing together. Call me when you can. Sean.*

"So who is this Sean?"

Now it was DJ's turn to blush. She could feel the heat creeping up her neck. "A friend I met at a drawing class."

"A friend, eh?" Karen looked back at the front of the card. "I'd say he's quite an artist already."

"He is." And a good friend, too. DJ closed her eyes for a moment. *Will I ever draw again?* From the look of her hands right now, both drawing and riding seemed utter impossibilities. She swallowed hard and opened her eyes. "You have to tell me about your date, promise?"

"I will."

That night, just before DJ went to sleep, two people holding hands snuck into her room.

"Karen, what. . . ?"

"Hi. Karen said you wanted to know how our date went." Allen White looked as handsome and nice in the dim light as before.

"Well, I mean, I . . ."

"Look at that, DJ can't think of anything to say." Karen giggled and patted DJ's leg.

"I can think of something." Allen gave Karen a look that said more than all his words. "Thanks, DJ, for making her go out with me. If it hadn't been for you, I never would have met her."

DJ swallowed past the lump in her throat. "Could you hand me a drink, please?"

Exactly two weeks later, DJ went home. The skin grafts took and were spreading. The new artificial skin they used worked even better than her own skin taken from her lower back. The list of instructions was longer than her arm, and she was scheduled for more cleansing treatments at the John Muir Medical Center, only a twenty-minute drive from her house.

Though DJ slept most of the way home, the walk from the car and up the stairs to her bedroom had her in near collapse by the time she could crawl into her own bed.

She stared around the room at all the signs and posters welcoming her home. "Wow. Who did all that?"

"Bobby and Billy did some."

"I can tell theirs."

"And each of the rest of us, and Amy and Shawna, and the one with the paw prints you can guess."

"How'd they get Queenie to walk in red paint?"

"It wasn't easy." Lindy shuddered. "Took two hours to scrub the paint off the deck."

"Where are the boys?"

"At Gran's. Joe has them hog-tied over there so we can get you settled in first. Then he'll let them loose." Robert brought in a box with more of her treasures from the hospital. Most of her balloons that hadn't deflated she'd sent to the pediatric ward or given to others on her floor. The bear and the fireman's hat sat on the bed beside her.

DJ leaned back against a mound of pillows. "I'm so glad to be home." She'd been in the hospital for more than a month.

Lindy sat down on the bed beside her daughter. "I was beginning to think the hospital was home. At least now you'll be able to sleep without people waking you all night."

"Mom, are you sure we can do this? I mean, I take a lot of taking care of."

"We'll hire help if we need to. Maria says she can sleep on a mattress here in your room if we need her to. She was all ready to move her bed up here yesterday."

"She is so good to me." DJ rolled her bottom lip. "How . . . I mean, what if I have to go to the bathroom in the night?"

"See this?" Lindy pointed to a box sitting on the edge of DJ's desk. "This is a baby intercom set up so we can hear in our bedroom. We'll put a speaker in the kitchen, too."

"A baby intercom?"

"Parents usually hang this on a crib so they can hear what the baby is doing when they are in another part of the house."

"Fifteen years old, and I've got a baby intercom."

"The boys were using it to call Queenie. It about drove her nuts."

No matter how tired she was, DJ could feel a giggle rising. Leave it to her two little brothers.

"Speaking of the angels . . ." Lindy pushed herself upright. "Here they come."

"DJ! DJ!" Their yells preceded them, as did feet pounding up the stairs. Despite GJ's injunctions to slow down, they plowed to a stop at the door. Lindy stood right in the middle of it.

"Okay, what are the rules?"

"Don't bump DJ's hands. Stay off the bed."

"And?"

Silence. DJ could picture their puzzled faces as they tried to remember what the third rule was.

"That's right. Be quiet." Lindy stepped aside, and the two tiptoed into the room until they saw DJ and, matching shrieks, broke loose. They planted hands on hips and their feet at the edge of the bed.

"We missed you. Are you all better? Did you see Queenie? Can we bring General up to see you? Can you come to the barn?" Their words tumbled faster, accelerating like a wagon rolling downhill.

"How come you're wearing balloons on your hands? Do you like our signs? Can you play checkers? Grandpa taught us to play checkers."

DJ didn't answer but just enjoyed the onslaught of questions.

"Mommy, can we go get Queenie? She's crying."

"She can wait in the garage a few more minutes."

"She missed DJ, too. Do your hands hurt bad?" They both leaned against the bed, one of them stroking DJ's arm, the other shaking his head, his round blue eyes bright with tears as he looked at her hands and her fuzzy head. "I'm sorry, DJ."

"Hey, guys, you didn't do anything. Here, one at a time, stand still and let me hug you. But you have to stand still." They both nodded, eyes rounder as they watched DJ scoot closer to them. Holding her hands up, she hugged each one with her elbows and upper arms.

"You boys can be a big help to DJ," Lindy said. "I'll teach you how to hold her glass to give her a drink of water, and you can even turn the pages of her school books so she can read her homework."

DJ groaned and the boys giggled.

"Okay, guys, let's go help Gran and Maria bring the food over." Robert winked at DJ and herded the boys out the door. "See you in a bit. We'll set up the picnic in here unless you'd rather come down to the deck."

DJ thought of the stairs and shook her head. No way could she make it down and then up again, no matter how much she'd rather eat out on the deck under the oak tree.

"Good. You take a quick nap and we'll see you in a bit."

"You need anything else?" Lindy moved the TV table closer to the bed. "You know, I think we should rent one of those tables that fit across the bed like they have at the hospital. Might make it easier for you."

"Thanks, Mom. I'm so glad to be home." DJ closed her eyes. She could hear the boys and their father downstairs. They must have let Queenie out of the garage, because she was no longer barking. All the sounds of home. *Thank you, God, I'm home.*

DJ felt her mother kiss her cheek, but she couldn't even open her eyes, they were so heavy.

When the screams woke DJ up, a night-light glowed from her bathroom.

7

"DJ, WHAT IS IT?"

"What's wrong?"

Her mother and father burst into her room in the same heartbeat.

"H-how'd you know?" DJ sucked in a deep breath, which brought on only a minor coughing spasm. She sat up straighter to ease the congestion.

"The baby monitor, remember?" Lindy glanced up at Robert, who stood beside her. "Why don't you get a warm washcloth?" She sat down on the bed and stroked DJ's leg through the cover. "What happened?"

"A nightmare, that's all." DJ could feel sweat trickle down her back and sides. Her insides were still shaking and her heart was thumping like it might jump out of her chest. "I get them a lot."

"Do you remember them when you wake up?" Lindy took the cloth Robert offered and wiped DJ's face and neck.

"Thanks, that feels good."

Robert sat beside her and began kneading her neck and shoulders.

"It's always horses, people screaming. And like I'm stuck in mud and can't get there to help them. I try and then I'm screaming, and then I wake up."

"Is there fire?"

"Uh-huh. But not always. It's just that I can't get there."

"What would you do if you could get there?"

"Beats me. I'm just stuck. Sometimes something is coming after me, and while I can't see it, I know it's there." She rotated her head from side to side and forward. "That feels so good."

"I'm sure the stuck feeling comes from where you are right now—stuck in bed, in therapy. Dreams are often reflections of where we are or something that is happening." Lindy wiped DJ's face and neck, then dried them with the towel Robert had brought with the washcloth. "How about a drink, too? The doctor said we have to push fluids since you aren't on the IV any longer."

DJ leaned into Robert's ministering fingers as she sucked on the straw. She glanced over at her lighted radio clock. "What happened to the picnic?"

"Sorry, but you were sleeping so soundly I couldn't bear to wake you up, so we ate outside. Think you can go back to sleep now?"

"Yes, thanks." DJ flopped back on her pillows and scooted down some in the bed. "Sorry I woke you."

"We're here for you, DJ. Just call and we'll come runnin'—waddling, in your mother's case."

"All right, Robert dear, you get to have the next one and see how well you do." Lindy took his hand to pull her to her feet. "Sometimes I think I must be carrying triplets."

"Really?" DJ could feel her mouth drop open.

"No. As far as we can tell, there is just one. He or she just plans on being toddler-size and ready to join a soccer team the minute it's born." Lindy held out the glass again. "You want another night-light in here or the hall light left on?"

"No, thanks. The dark feels good after all the lights and noise at the hospital."

"Amy called," Lindy said when DJ wandered slowly into the kitchen for breakfast. "She's coming over after school on her way to Briones."

"Here, you sit." Maria set a tall glass of fresh-from-the-squeezer orange juice with a straw in it on the table. "Got to get some meat on your bones again." With her dark hair, dark eyes, and flashing smile, Maria patted DJ's shoulder as she went by. "So good to have you home. Get good care, now."

DJ sat and inhaled the orange juice. At least she could drink without help if a straw was available. She leaned back in the chair and watched the hummingbirds at the feeders out on the deck while Maria cut up sausages and buttered toast. "Will we be home by the time Amy comes by?"

"Should be." Lindy fed DJ and ate her own breakfast at the same time. "How'd you sleep?"

"Good." DJ tried to stop a yawn, but it got by her. "Sorry."

Lindy caught it and almost missed DJ's mouth with the fork, her own yawn so wide it shut her eyes. "Stop that."

Oh man, I'm so glad to be home. Thank you, God. Thank you, thank you, thank you.

After breakfast, DJ went back upstairs and, with Lindy's help, struggled into real clothes for her trip to the new doctor.

At the John Muir Medical Center, they met Dr. Arm-stadt, DJ's new therapists, both physical and occupational, the scrub team—or as DJ called them to her mother, the "killer team"—and several others whose names DJ forgot as soon as they said them. But the routine remained the same, and DJ still hadn't gotten used to the pain—never did, never would, and couldn't wait until it wouldn't happen anymore.

Dr. Armistadt said the scrub treatments would taper off now.

She knew she'd like the man.

DJ was sound asleep when Amy arrived that afternoon, but she had made her mother promise to wake her up.

"Hey, sleepyhead, you want to go riding?"

"Hi, Amy." DJ blinked several times, as usual wishing she could rub her eyes.

"Kids are asking about you at school." Amy sat cross-legged on the end of DJ's bed.

DJ sat up and copied the action. "I'll be getting a tutor soon." She made a face. "Did you get into that photography class?"

"Did I ever. But I already know most of the camera stuff. We start in the darkroom next week. That'll be way cool." Amy cocked her head. Her dark hair had been brushed to the side and tied into a low ponytail that fell over her right shoulder. "Your hair is getting longer. Looks cute."

"Thanks. Short like this is easy to wash, that's for sure."

"When are you coming over to the barns?"

DJ shrugged. "Soon, I guess." She propped her elbows on her knees. "So tell me what's going on over there."

"Western show on Saturday, so we're getting ready for that. Joe says he's not taking Ranger until the trainer works more with them together." Ranger was Joe's young cutting horse. "The last show, Joe almost went one way and Ranger the other."

"So?"

The two girls giggled at that one.

"I better head over there. I need to work on Josh's tail, and the farrier is supposed to be there at 4:30. See ya."

When Amy left, DJ settled back against her pillows. Did

she really want to go to the barns? Ignoring the answer, she fell back asleep.

The next few days slipped into a rhythm. DJ was feeling better in the mornings, even up to doing homework. They'd drive to Walnut Creek for treatments at the John Muir Medical Center in the afternoon. She was doped up pretty well for the treatments and, once home, slept on into the evening.

On Friday they showed DJ how well the skin grafts were growing. She nearly gagged, but pure fascination made her study what her therapist, Jody, was telling her.

"See, here we have your own skin from between your fingers where the damage wasn't as great. Here are the grafts, and this part over here is where we used the artificial skin grown in a lab. It works like a net for your own skin cells to grow over more quickly. Since we were able to keep infection from setting in, the tissue is responding more quickly. But we have to keep the tendons from tightening your fingers into claws, and keep the skin from growing into a web between your fingers. All that means working the hands, no matter how much it hurts."

DJ shuddered. "Nothing can be worse than the scrubbing."

"So they say. I know this doesn't look real good to you right now, but trust me, you're coming along famously."

DJ could feel her face grow hot.

"Are you eating all right?"

"When I'm awake. After the treatments I sleep right through dinner, but Mom brings me a tray."

"Get lots of fruit and vegetables. They'll help you feel better all around. And get up and walk." Jody checked her chart. "You still get dizzy?"

"Some."

"Okay, then have someone walk with you. The more you can get out in the sunshine, the better. Just keep the hands clean. That's one reason we still bandage them. Keeping them clean and dry is imperative."

"Am I ever going to be able to take a shower again?"

"Sure. Just bag your hands in plastic, tape them shut, and hold them up out of the water. One good thing is you don't have to wash your hair every day." Jody stepped back. "Not many people can go with their hair so short, but on you it looks good. Would you rather use a wig?"

"No, hats are fine. My grandma found me a couple that work okay. Maybe when it's a bit longer I won't feel like I need a bag for my head."

"Trust me, kid. If I looked as good as you, I'd wear my hair that short all the time. So easy to care for."

As they always did after the treatments, DJ and her mom stopped by the ice cream parlor to get her a jamoca almond malt—large size to go.

"Mmm. This is so good. What if I become a malt addict?" DJ opened her eyes again after closing them in delight.

"Beats drugs, that's for sure." Lindy watched the light, waiting for the green.

"Mom?"

"What, dear?"

"I won't be a drug addict when this is over, will I?"

"The doctors don't think so. Dr. Niguri said that they'll wean you off the morphine now as this other pain-killer takes effect. It's one of those that takes time to build up to an effective level in the bloodstream. He said you will feel more alert, but that rest is still really important."

"I can't keep it all straight."

"That's okay. It gives the rest of us something to do."

"Jody said I can take a shower if we bag my hands."

"Good. That alone should make you feel better."

DJ watched the scenery go by, but before they reached Pleasant Hill, her eyes had drifted closed. She had a hard time waking up enough to get out of the car and up the stairs to her room, where she sat down on the bed and fell over asleep. She vaguely heard Maria *tsk*-ing as she lifted DJ's legs and swung them up on the bed. *Thank you.* But the words never made it to audible level.

"Hey, darlin', how you doin'?" Gran breezed into DJ's room Monday morning with her normal collection of baggage.

DJ shrugged and tried to blink to clear her eyes, which had been closed instead of focused on her schoolwork. "Just can't keep awake."

"This, too, shall pass. The Bible promises." While Gran spoke, she pulled two garments from her bag and held them up. "What do you think?"

DJ shrugged again.

"I designed them myself. See . . . wide, loose sleeves to go over your bandages, elastic around the neck, so no buttons. We can just pull them over your head and voila, you are dressed. Pure comfort. No shorts to pull up and down, and no more living in nightgowns or those ugly hospital gowns." Gran leaned over and whispered, "And you don't even have to wear a bra."

Like I really need one. "Thanks." *How do I tell her these are like old lady dresses?*

"Now, I know these aren't the fashion statement of the day, but jeans are hard to get on and off, and those tiny T-shirts won't go over—"

"My boxing gloves, I know."

"Well, you give them a try, and we'll modify the pattern if we think of something else that will work. Here, I'll help you put one on now."

DJ kept her expression noncommittal only with great

effort. *Gran, you know I don't wear dresses.* But she held up her arms to make it easier for Gran to slip the garment over her head.

"I can put elastic around the waist if you like, or we can do a belt." Gran pulled a belt made of braided strips of fabric from her bag and held it around DJ's waist. "Oh my, darlin', you've lost a lot of weight. I measured this off your jeans."

"She not lose more. I make sure of that." Maria stood in the doorway, hands on hips and nodding. "That looks good, and comfortable, too. Did it hurt your hands?"

DJ shook her head, surprised at herself. She'd been concentrating so hard on the fit that she'd forgotten about her boxing gloves. She stared at the person in the mirror. The turquoise material made her eyes look greener than ever and her fuzzy hair blonder. Looking taller than she remembered being, DJ was skinny now, not just straight.

"Sheesh, maybe I should be a model. My neck is long enough for a goose. I bet my jeans are gonna just fall off. What do you think, Queenie?"

The black-and-white dog raised her head from where she lay snoozing on the bed. She cocked her head to one side, gave a little *woof*, and laid her head back on her paws.

"Was that a yes?" One eyebrow went up. "Guess so."

"No. I fix, you eat. I feed you up good." Maria walked around her. "I think you look good in that. Nice legs. You wear skirts and dresses more often." Her dark eyes flashed. "Boys come all time then."

"She's too young for boys." Gran evened out the gathers on the dress and stood back. "Looks nice, Darla Jean. You want any changes?"

"Jeans?"

Gran rolled her eyes. "I'm thinking of making a short-sleeved top and elastic-waist shorts for when you leave the house."

"That would be cool. Thank you for sewing them for me." DJ dropped a kiss on her grandmother's head. "Not like you had tons of time, I know."

"You come down now for lunch?" Maria paused in the doorway.

"I just had breakfast."

"You eat before leave for hospital. Made chocolate chip mint cookies just for you."

"That was what smelled so good. You think maybe you could fix up a plate for me to take to Jody? Maybe if I bribe her she'll go easier on me today."

"Fat chance." Gran hung the other dress up in DJ's closet and pulled shorts and a tank top from a drawer.

"Sure, I do that. You hurry down now."

"Okay, thanks. Just let me get my clothes on." DJ looked around for her sandals. "At least I don't have to brush my hair."

"That's my girl." Gran gave her an around-the-waist hug. "Let's get you ready."

After a lunch of grilled tuna sandwiches and chips, with a banana smoothie to drink, Gran and DJ got ready to leave.

"You think something is wrong that Mom's taking so long?" DJ asked. Lindy had a doctor's appointment in the morning and had said she should be back in time but, just in case, Gran would fill in.

"No, she had some errands to run, too. We can call her on the cell phone if you want."

"No, that's okay. Got the cookies?"

Gran nodded. "And a water bottle. Anything else?"

"Nope. See ya, Maria."

On Friday DJ was making her way down the stairs when the doorbell rang. "I'll get it," she yelled without thinking. Not looking down, she picked up her pace. Her foot landed wrong, and the stairs came up to meet her.

"My hands!" Her scream broke halfway down.

8

"DARLA JEAN, ARE YOU ALL RIGHT?"

The doorbell rang again.

"Coming, just a minute!" Lindy yelled at the door and gathered a sobbing DJ into her arms. "Are you hurt anywhere?"

"Just my hands. Oh, Mom, it hurts so bad." DJ sat on the lower step, her elbows resting on her knees, hands in the air. "I slammed them against the stairs. I tried twisting to the side, but . . ."

Queenie licked away her tears as fast as they fell. She whimpered and glued herself to DJ's side.

"At least you didn't break anything. Don't move. Let me get the door."

DJ tried to stifle her sobs by taking deep breaths. If only she could at least blow her own nose! She started to get up but sat down just as abruptly. Her ankle screamed at her when she put weight on it. The thought of not being able to walk made her cry even harder. Queenie crawled under DJ's arm and halfway onto her lap, her tongue still on tear patrol.

She could hear her mother at the door. It was a delivery of some sort.

"I heard a scream. Can I help you, ma'am?" The deep

voice obviously belonged to a man.

"I . . . ah . . . my daughter took a tumble on the stairs." Lindy looked over her shoulder to see DJ wincing when she tried rotating her ankle. "Yes, maybe you can. Come in, please."

"I . . . I'm sorry, Mom, but I hurt my ankle, too." The tears continued to roll in spite of everything DJ tried to stop them.

"Hey, you look like you're in a world of hurt." The tall man in khaki shirt and shorts set a flower arrangement down on the table by the door. "Are you DJ?"

"Mm-hmm." DJ sniffed.

"The flowers are for you, but it looks like what you need is a strong arm to help you to a chair."

Another sniff. "I guess. What a stupid thing to do." Queenie curled her upper lip at the man towering over them. DJ hugged her close and whispered in her ear, "Easy, girl, it's all right. He's trying to help us."

"That's why they're called accidents. My name is John." He turned to Lindy. "Where do you want her?"

"On the sofa in the family room, please." She pointed through the arch.

"Okay. You call off the dog and we'll take care of this."

"Queenie, here girl." Lindy slapped her thigh.

Queenie gave her a look that clearly said, "You have got to be kidding. My job is here with DJ." She glanced up at the man and showed her teeth again, but very politely this time.

"Queenie, it's all right. Go on, go with Mom." The dog's look clearly said that she disagreed with this order but would obey if they insisted. They did.

"Good dog you have there." John leaned forward and put his arm around DJ's waist. "Okay, on three. One, two, three." He heaved, DJ braced on her good foot, and she was upright again, her arms held in toward her body to protect her hands. "You know, it might be easier if I just carried you."

"I . . . I'm pretty big." DJ could feel her face flaming like she'd fallen asleep under a sun lamp.

"Not quite. Looks like half a wind could blow you over."

"Took less than that on the stairs." At least she could talk now without sobbing.

"Okay, so you hold your hands out and I'll do the rest." With the ease of a man used to heavy lifting, John swung her up in his arms without even a grunt and within strides deposited her on the sofa. "Now, how's that?"

"Good."

"I'll get some ice for that ankle." Lindy turned toward the kitchen. "John, can I get you something to drink or—"

"No, thanks. Got to get on my route. Mind me asking what happened to your hands?"

"Burned them in a barn." DJ leaned against the back of the couch, her injured foot resting on the cushion. "All I needed was to hurt another part of me."

"Yeah, bummer." He left the room and returned with the bouquet of red carnations and white chrysanthemums in a rough twig basket. A red *Get Well* balloon bobbed above its anchor on the handle of the basket. "Here ya go. You can at least enjoy these." He handed her the card.

"Thanks for your help."

"You are more than welcome. This was easy. One day I came to a house to find a woman in labor and made a flying run with her to the hospital. Almost had to deliver a baby. I've had first aid and CPR training, but not midwifery—first thing I thought of when your mother answered the door."

Lindy set the blue ice bag on DJ's ankle and walked John to the door, thanking him profusely all the way. When she returned, she wrapped a towel around the bag to hold it in place and put a pillow under the foot. "Ice and elevate." She stood back. "I sure hope you didn't break something." She glanced at her watch. "I think I better call Joe to come help us get you to treatment."

"Can't I skip?"

"Nope. And this way we can get your ankle checked at the same time."

"Could you please wash my face? My eyes feel like they have rocks in them." She knew her tone of voice left a lot to be desired, but right now anything more was beyond her ability. She could hear Gran's voice reminding her to thank God in all things, but that seemed impossible, too.

DJ came home from the hospital groggy as always, but this time with a tightly wrapped foot, due to a minor sprain, and a frown the size of New Hampshire. As Robert helped DJ into the house and to a chair, the boys came running. They wore matching round eyes.

"What happened to your foot?" Once again in unison. One of them—in her befuddled and muddled state DJ wasn't sure which and at the moment didn't much care to know—reached out to touch her propped-up, swollen, and wrapped foot.

"Don't!"

"Sorry." Immediately all four blue eyes filled with tears.

DJ felt so low, the belly of a turtle would be far beyond her reach. *What a creep you are. They didn't do anything.* "I'm sorry, guys." She glanced up to see tears in her mother's eyes.

She held out her arms on either side of the chair. "Come here. Just watch out for the hands and foot, okay? I hurt at both ends."

"Your hands, DJ—no bandages." The boys took on their wide-eyed look again.

"I know. Cool gloves, huh?" With one twin on each side

of her, their elbows propped on the arms of her chair and their eyes magically clearing to their usual summer-sky blue, DJ hugged them, careful to keep her gloved hands out of the way. "Please forgive me for being such a grouch?"

"You're a hurting grouch, huh?" one of the boys said as Queenie put her front paws on the knee of DJ's good leg.

"Sure am." She blinked hard. Medication took the terrible pain out of her hands, but keeping her eyes open and her chin off her chest still took all the energy she possessed. Not that she had that much.

"Okay, guys—let's get DJ upstairs," Robert said. Though DJ was capable of hobbling with a little help, Robert swung her up in his arms and grunted his way up the stairs.

Once DJ was on her bed, tears of self-pity leaked from her eyes in spite of her sniffing.

Queenie jumped up on the bed and gave her a quick slurp. DJ buried her face in the dog's fur, ashamed to look at her dad. After he'd done so much to try to make things easier for her, all she could do was sound like a permanent grouch.

"Just call me Oscar," she muttered.

Robert sat down on the edge of the bed. "It's okay, DJ. You're entitled to a bout of self-pity. Seems to me you've handled all this far better than most fifteen-year-old kids would. I think if it were me, I'd pull the covers over my head and tell the entire world to take a hike. A l-o-n-g hike. You sleep for a while and perhaps things will look better when you wake up. I'll get the intercom set up again so we can hear if you holler for help."

"Thanks, Dad." She felt his kiss on her cheek. Queenie lay within the curve of her arm, and they sighed matching sighs.

For a change, DJ woke in time for dinner. Robert helped her back downstairs and out to the deck to join the family. Sparrows and finches chattered in the oak tree that sheltered much of the deck in the evening. The hummingbirds ignored the family around the table and continued to dive and display at the two glass feeders hung on wrought-iron hooks off the deck railing. Their squeaks and clicks and the humming of their wings were part of the deck music, along with the hiss of the sprinklers and an occasional shout from a neighbor's yard.

DJ studied the roses that bloomed along the deck, the pots full of bright pink and white begonias, and the blue stalks of salvia as if she'd never seen them before. A bird-house hung from one of the oak branches, and peanut shells told where the squirrels had dined on the deck railing.

"General wants to tell you hi, too." One of the twins leaned on the arm of her chair. DJ had been giving the boys riding lessons on their pony before she was injured. "Grandpa Joe helped us when you were gone."

"We missed you something awful." The other twin had taken up the other arm.

"All right, you two. Who's who?" DJ looked from one round, smiling face to the other. No bandages or bruises to tell them apart.

"I got a loose tooth, see?" The twin on her right side wiggled an upper front tooth.

DJ pointed to his chest. "Name?"

"Bobby."

"So Billy doesn't have a loose tooth yet?"

Billy shook his head as if he were on the wrong end of a tragedy. "Nuh-uh. Not fair." He pinched a tooth between thumb and finger and tried in vain to move it. "Thee?"

"Have you boys washed your hands?" Lindy set a bowl full of tossed salad on the table.

Both boys raised their hands and flipped them front and back.

"What about faces?" They darted off to the bathroom,

giggling as they went. Queenie chased after them, a sharp *yip* cheering them on. "Would you rather sit on the lounger?" Lindy came over and stroked DJ's fuzzy hair.

DJ shook her head and leaned into her mother's caress. "Then I can't eat at the table. Mom, it is so beautiful out here and smells heavenly." She inhaled a long, appreciative sniff.

"That's the roses and the alyssum. The lemon tree is blooming, too. In fact, we'll get to pick our first lemon pretty soon. The blossom end of it is still pretty green. . . .

"Ah, DJ, you have no idea how much we've all missed you," Lindy continued. "Nothing has been the same with you gone. What with you at USET camp back east, then straight to the horse show, and then the hospital, it seems like you've been gone forever. And to think . . ." Lindy stopped and cleared her throat. "We came so close to losing you. I just can't thank God enough for letting you stay here with us."

"Me too." DJ blew out her cheeks, the exhaled breath whistling through pursed lips.

"Okay, Deej, we did it." Robert bounded up the stairs from the lower level of the redwood deck to the top. He held out a spoon and a fork with handles made fat with foam rubber. "This way you can grip them whether your fingers want to clamp or not." He held the utensils up to be seen more easily. "You can make about anything with foam rubber and duct tape."

"Gorgeous." Lindy inspected the contraptions.

"Dinner ready." Maria stopped in the open doorway. "You do good, Mr. Robert. Now DJ can feed herself."

"Not that we mind helping you." Lindy took the fork and placed the handle against DJ's right gloved palm. "Now, see if you can close your fingers around it."

DJ focused all her will on her stiffly stretched fingers. *Come on, bend. Hang on to the fork. Bend!* Her forefinger moved the most, but only slightly, so Lindy cupped her hand over the back of DJ's and gently pressed the fingers inward.

DJ flinched and swallowed against the pain. But the hurt was nothing like it used to be, and her hands had to learn to work again. She concentrated on keeping hold of the fork, but it fell in her lap. A groan seeped from between her clenched teeth.

"No, not to worry. Each day will get better." Robert worked her hand this time, pressing each finger to curve around the handle. Again the fork fell.

"Maybe we should tape the fork to her glove."

"No, but how about elastic? Then it would have some give."

While the two of them discussed solutions, DJ stared at her gloved hands. If she couldn't even hold a padded fork, how was she ever going to be able to hold two reins and feel the tender mouth of her mount?

"Darla Jean, your tutor will be here about eleven. The school just called," Lindy announced the following Monday.

DJ kept the groan inside. The last thing she wanted to do was meet her tutor; the first thing she wanted to do was fall back asleep. The night had been rugged enough, what with two nightmares and needing to take pain pills in the middle of the night.

"But I don't have my homework caught up yet." Whoops, not a good thing to say. The look she got said, "So whose fault is that?" Her mom just didn't get it. Why read something when it went out of your brain faster than your eyes could put it in? Or your ears, since she was still working on the book report on *Tom Sawyer*. DJ sighed. At least she didn't have therapy today. Here she thought she'd have a free day—to sleep.

Slipping into sleep was one of the things she did best, even though lots of times she didn't get to stay that way long.

"Wouldn't you rather meet with her out on the deck?" Lindy glanced around DJ's room, and the furrow between her eyes showed what she thought of it. DJ didn't have to look. She knew a slob had moved in, but shouldn't a patient be allowed to be a bit messy when things were so hard to pick up?

"I guess." DJ swung her legs to the side of the bed and stood up, still hesitating before moving again in case the dizziness came back. Bending over still caused the room to spin at times, so things lay on the floor where she dropped them. She'd just gotten herself downstairs and settled on the deck with a strawberry-banana smoothie when she heard the doorbell ring. Most likely she should have brought her books down with her.

Lindy brought their guest out and sat down across the table.

"Hi, DJ, I'm Debra Allendra. You may call me Debra if you like, or Ms. Allendra if you prefer."

DJ glanced from the slim young woman with sparkling eyes to her mother, who shrugged. Since when did teachers want to go by their first name? "Glad to meet you." *Liar. This is about as bad as a new therapist.*

"Would you like something to drink?" Lindy asked as Ms. Allendra removed some papers from her briefcase and took a seat next to DJ's.

"Sure, thanks. Anything is fine."

"Iced tea?"

"Great." She turned to DJ. "Okay, so why don't we start with you telling me what happened and how you're doing with the lessons that have been sent home for you."

Does she really want to know, or do I be polite and keep it short? In as few words as possible, DJ filled her in on the accident, the hospital, getting home, and her drained brain. "So I get further behind every day and . . ." She trailed off into a shrug and took a long drink of her smoothie, using both hands at the wrists to hold the glass.

Debra nodded and spoke words of encouragement throughout DJ's rundown, then said, "I see. Looks to me like fighting the brain drain will have to be a major focus for us." She glanced down at her notes. "I think a normal plan of studies is beyond you right now, so let's decide on an easier track for a week or two, then increase the work load as you are able. But you have to promise me you will try your hardest, or I'll be all over you like a dog after a flea." She flashed a smile that made DJ nod in return.

Trying hard seemed beyond her at the moment, but Gran kept saying that things would get better soon. It was just that *soon* seemed a long time coming.

9

"CAN I TRUST YOU to do the work on your own?"

DJ stared at her physical therapist, Jody. *Does she think I'm dumb? Of course I'll work on my own. I have to be able to use my hands—yesterday.*

"I think for DJ the opposite is more true. How much is too much?" Gran laid a hand on DJ's shoulder as they both looked at the therapist.

"The old adage is to let the pain be your guide." Jody pushed against DJ's fingers to determine their strength. "If you find the pain in your hands wakes you up in the night, you've overdone it that day. But the more you stretch them, the better. Use the ball, see, and squeeze like this. It helps to have someone else keep pushing your fingers in." Again she showed DJ how by folding each finger, one at a time, in toward the palm of her hand.

"Now, how's your ankle?"

"Better. It's been a week since I hurt it."

"Good. Soak it in a whirlpool if you can."

DJ nodded. "I have a Jacuzzi at home."

"Good. Then put your foot on one of the jets and let the pulsing water massage it. Also, the more you keep your ankle up—and by *up* I mean higher than your heart—the better. If you can keep the swelling down, it will heal faster."

All the while Jody was talking, DJ kept putting the backs of her fingers against the tabletop and pushing so that her fingers had to curve in.

"How are you doing with your tutor?"

DJ shrugged. "I'm so far behind I don't know how I'll ever catch up."

"You will. Now, do you have any other questions?"

DJ shook her head.

"Okay, then I'll see you tomorrow."

Over the next few days, DJ found it easier and easier to lie back on her bed and fall asleep. When she woke up, she felt groggy and grumpy, so unless someone woke her or called her to meals or she talked on the phone, sleeping felt much better. When she slept, she didn't have to think or feel at all.

"DJ! Are you sleeping again?" Lindy stood in the doorway to the deck.

"Uh . . . no. I just closed my eyes for a minute." DJ blinked and yawned, a dead giveaway.

"Do you hurt? I mean, any more than normal?" Lindy crossed to the lounger and laid the back of her hand on DJ's forehead.

DJ kept her head still with some effort. Sometimes she just needed to be alone. "Mom, I'm fine, okay?"

"Yeah, right." Lindy huffed a sigh.

DJ heard her muttering as she returned to the kitchen.

The next few days passed in a blur, and all DJ knew at the end of each day was that she could never see much of an improvement in the way her fingers moved. Stiff and unyielding they stayed, no matter how much she tried bending them.

"I'm coming. I'm coming!" DJ pulled the blanket back

up over her ears in response to her mother's yell up the stairs Thursday morning. If she didn't open her eyes, she didn't have to admit morning had come. She drifted back to that land of fuzzy gray.

"Darla Jean Randall, get out of that bed!" Lindy yanked the covers back. Her tone of voice allowed no arguments.

DJ reached for the covers, but her fingers wouldn't close enough to grasp them. "In a minute, okay? Mom, I am so tired."

"I know it seems that way, but sleeping all the time is a strong indication of depression. Mother and I talked it over and we're pretty sure that's what's happening with you. You were doing so well, and now that you are better physically, you sleep more than ever."

"No, I don't!" DJ swung her feet over the edge of the bed. "Why can't you just leave me alone?"

"How late did you study last night?"

DJ flinched. The last time she'd looked at the clock was 8:30, and she was pretty sure she'd fallen asleep shortly after that. She squinted to see the clock. It was 10:30. No wonder her mother was on a rampage.

"Debra will be here in fifteen minutes."

DJ groaned again. She'd planned on finishing her assignments this morning. "Can't you call her and . . ." She glanced at her mother and wisely cut off her request. No, there'd be no calling to cancel, not this late, anyway.

"You already canceled yesterday."

"All right. I'll be ready." DJ heaved herself to her feet and hobbled into her bathroom. When she looked in the mirror, she wished she hadn't. There were black, puffy circles under her eyes, and what hair she had was in mats and spikes. How long since she'd washed it? Or taken a shower?

"Do you want me to help you?"

"No—I mean no, thank you." She'd taken to leaving the

cap off the toothpaste tube so she could squeeze some on her fat-handled toothbrush.

Lindy *humph*ed from the doorway and spun on her heel. "You have not quite ten minutes."

DJ stuck her head under the faucet since there was no time for a shower. Oh, for the days when she could shower, including washing her long hair, and dress in ten minutes. Now even applying deodorant was a major effort. So she didn't. She rubbed her wet head with a towel, brushed her teeth, and pulled over her head one of the big shirts Gran had sewn for her.

Her stomach rumbled at the same time she heard the front doorbell chime. She threw her bedcovers up so it didn't look so bad; kicking yesterday's clothes under the bed helped, too.

"Hi, DJ, how are you doing?" Debra Allendra stopped in the doorway, her smile perky as usual.

Just great, can't you tell? "Fine." DJ glanced around to see the furrow deepen between her mother's eyebrows. Lindy had walked the tutor to the bedroom door. *Uh-oh, in for it again.* DJ gritted her teeth. If only they'd all leave her alone. Her mother was turning into a permanent grouch. *If she doesn't get off my back . . .*

DJ ambled over to her desk and picked up her books to spread them on the bed.

"Would you like something to drink?" Lindy offered.

Yeah, like she'll bring me something to drink. The day before, Lindy had announced that she and Maria were no longer bringing food and drinks up to DJ's room. She had to come down for them herself.

"Iced tea would be great. Thank you." Debra pulled up a chair and set her bag by her feet. "So our time is flying by. Let's get on with it."

DJ plunked down on the bed.

"Let's go over the checklist." Debra tucked her chin-length dark hair behind her right ear and set her clipboard on her lap. "Did you finish your book report?"

DJ shook her head. "You know how hard it is to turn pages, and when I listen to the audio, I fall asleep." *Not a good answer. Who cares?*

"Hmm." Debra rolled her bottom lip in, then looked up at DJ. "Where were you listening to the tape?"

DJ studied her gloves. "On the bed." *Why can't I lie and say at the desk or outside or something?*

"Maybe the bed's part of the problem. Sitting up in a chair might help that. How many hours did you try?"

DJ shrugged.

Debra ran through the rest of her checklist, which had marks in only four of the boxes. She laid the clipboard in front of DJ. "Not too good, huh?"

DJ clamped her teeth. Tracing circles on her duvet took all her attention.

"DJ, do you want to flunk this semester?"

"No, I just can't study!" With one hand she swept the papers off her bed and watched them flutter to the floor. "Why does everybody have to keep after me like this?"

"Because no matter how badly one is hurt, you have to pick up your life again and keep going. Because people care, and because we all know that the longer you stay down, the longer it will take to get your life back."

DJ raised her hands in the air. "But what if I never get it back? What if my hands never work like they used to? What if I can't draw or ride? What if my hands always stay this ugly and . . ." She gritted her teeth against the tears. "I cry all the time and . . ." She dashed the tears away with the back of one hand. "And I can't concentrate. I read something, and two minutes later I can't remember what I read. Like there's a big hole in my brain that sucks it all in and it just disappears. I hate this!"

"DJ, I—"

"And everyone keeps picking at me. All I want to do is go riding, and I can't. I can't do anything I want to do." She could hear herself screaming but couldn't seem to stop. "It's not fair! I try and try and I'm not getting anywhere. Look at my hands. I still can't even hold my toothbrush."

The silence of the room screamed back at her.

"And now I've been a total idiot and I hate me, too." DJ threw herself across the bed and buried her face in the pillow. Maybe she would smother and all this would be over with. Everyone could go back to their regular lives and not be all messed up because of hers.

She felt Queenie jump up on the bed and come nuzzle under DJ's arm so she could lick away the tears. She whimpered deep in her throat, a crying sound that made DJ sob harder.

When she ran out of tears, she pushed herself upright and fumbled for a tissue. Several appeared in her hand as if by magic. She scrubbed her face with them, made a mess of blowing her nose but accomplished it anyway, and finally sat up facing the wall, away from her tutor.

"I . . . I'm sorry." *Mom's really going to have plenty to say now. What an idiot I am.*

"I'd say this has been building up for quite some time."

"I guess."

"Do you feel better?"

DJ took inventory. "I . . . I guess so." She did indeed, like maybe she could sit or stand straight instead of feeling as if the universe were pushing her down.

But her nose stung and her eyes burned.

She checked again. Yes, she did feel better. She sniffed and tossed the tissues in the wastebasket before reaching for more.

"Now, why don't you go wash your face in cool water and come back. You want some iced tea, too?"

"I guess." DJ limped into the bathroom and stared at the

balloon face in the mirror. What a mess. She pushed the lever to Cold and dropped a washcloth under the flow. Using both hands she lifted the soaking cloth and laid her face in it. Water ran down her arms and the front of her clothes. She squeezed the cloth out the best she could and draped it over the rod before drying her face on the towel.

Now if only she didn't have to face the tutor again. Maybe she could fly out the window or something.

Taking a deep breath and letting it out in a sigh, DJ returned to her bedroom.

Debra stood in front of the framed horse pictures, all DJ's own drawings and many of them the originals for the DJAM card line. She turned when she heard DJ returning.

"These are all yours?"

DJ nodded. "But it's not all that I've done. There are plenty more in there." She indicated the cabinet of wide, shallow drawers—enough to be the envy of many art teachers.

"I never had a chance to look so close before to see your signature. You have quite a studio here."

"I know. My dad and Gran designed this all just for me."

"They love you a great deal."

"I know. That's what makes my being such a brat so much worse."

"DJ, you are fifteen years old, you've had a terrible accident, and for a while life just isn't going to be the way you thought or planned. From everything I hear, you are one dedicated and determined young woman. But anyone can get depressed when facing the kind of obstacles you are." Debra shook her head. "I have a feeling that someday parts of this will become funny even. But right now, I know, not much seems funny to you. And the concentration thing? It's not unusual with head injuries. I know you don't want to hear me say that things could be so much worse, but really they could. Your mind will get its act back together, your hands will heal, and according to the doctor's report, they haven't even mentioned long-term disability. That's good, too." Debra tucked her hair behind her ear. "Your hands will work right again, and your mind will work right again. Please be patient with yourself. And let's keep you out of depression if we can."

DJ studied her gloved hands. *God, please make Debra right. I know I'm not doing good, but it is so hard.*

"D-do you like cards?" DJ had to clear her throat to get the words past the frog that tried to croak in her throat.

"I love cards. Why?"

"Because I'd like to give you a set. Pull out the third drawer."

Debra did and found packets of DJ's and Amy's cards in perfect order, ready to be shipped out. The young woman took up a package that was a mixture of photos and drawings. She untied the gift bow and looked at each card, smiling, nodding, and shaking her head.

"These are wonderful. Who is Amy Yamamoto?"

"My best friend. She shoots photos, I draw." *At least I used to*. DJ flexed her fingers and tried to clench them into a fist. "We needed to make some money, so . . ."

"Can I buy some?"

"I want to give you a packet."

"I know, but can I buy more? These would make great presents."

"I guess."

"Good." Debra chose another mixed pack and then one of each of the others. After looking from one pack to the other, she turned to look at DJ. "Have you ever thought of letting groups sell these for fund-raisers?"

DJ nodded.

"Good. Let me talk to my women's group. We're always looking for ways to make money, and if we can help a business owned by women, so much the better, especially very *young* women." She put the packets in her bag, counted out her money, and laid it on DJ's desk. "Now, let's get back to work. Since I didn't realize you were having memory trouble when I made these assignments, I'll revise the list before I come again. For now, I recommend that you study at your desk, sitting in your chair, to help you concentrate. No music or TV going during study time, and work in short bursts rather than long stretches. Taking deep breaths, like ten in a row, will help get more oxygen to your brain and help you think better. Get up and move around frequently." She leaned forward and touched DJ's arm. DJ looked into her teacher's eyes.

"And most importantly, you have to think *up*. Understand?"

DJ nodded.

"Good. Now, let's get to work on what we have."

By the time Debra left, DJ felt that maybe schoolwork wasn't the worst thing on the planet. At least she didn't have to do algebra this year.

Debra had just driven out of the yard when the doorbell rang again. Since DJ was downstairs, she answered it. "Bridget! Come in." She stepped back and motioned her coach, trainer, friend, employer—all of the above at various times in DJ's life—into the house.

"Hey, I like the new hairdo. Do you think short-short would look good on me?" Bridget gave DJ a hug and stepped back to look at her. "A rumor has made it to my attention, and I decided I had better come investigate."

DJ felt the flinch that started in her foot and worked itself to the tender tips of her fingers. "A rumor?" The frog had hopped back into her throat.

Bridget nodded, her blue eyes serious, although a slight crinkle at the outer edges told of her hours in the sun and an incipient smile.

"Come on out to the deck. Maria will bring us iced tea."

"I see you are walking well again."

"Umm . . . I guess." *What rumor? What did—or didn't—I do now?*

10

"IS IT ALL RIGHT if I steal away your daughter?" Bridget had tracked Lindy down in the kitchen.

Lindy nodded. "I guess, if you promise to bring her back."

"Eventually." Bridget finished the last swallow of her iced tea and nodded to DJ. "Come along, *ma petite*. I have something to show you."

Wish I dared to say no. All I want is a nap. Why am I so tired all the time? "Okay." You did not argue with Bridget. DJ had learned that long ago. And you didn't make excuses, either. That was a lesson she'd learned not so long ago.

"So how are you—really?" Bridget shifted gears and checked the traffic both ways while waiting for DJ to answer.

You mean after I just spent an hour screaming at my tutor, or do you mean in general? DJ almost said "Fine," but Bridget could pick up on a lie faster than DJ's mother could. By the time DJ had argued every side of the question, all without saying a word, a sigh escaped.

"Not good?"

"No, I mean yes." Though DJ had conquered the finger-nail-biting habit that had plagued her for years, right now she would have given anything to be able to chew her cuticles. That is, if she would ever have cuticles and finger-nails again. She curled and flexed her fingers, using the movement both as a distraction and because she knew it would help—eventually.

"Let me guess. You are scared you will not be able to ride again." Bridget glanced at DJ for confirmation.

DJ nodded.

"You are angry that your hands are not responding as fast as you think they should."

Another nod.

"Anything else?"

"What if I can't even draw?" DJ's voice squeaked on the final word.

"Of course, that, too. Anything else?"

DJ took in a deep breath and told Bridget about the session with her tutor.

"Ah, ma petite, do you still not know that you do not have to do it all alone? Talking this out with older and wiser heads is the only way to keep your sanity. Everyone who experiences major traumas and setbacks feels this way. It is normal. But withdrawing is the most dangerous of responses. I was hoping to see you at the barns by now, dreaming of riding, at least being with the other kids and the horses."

"It hurts too bad." DJ spoke into her shirt front.

"Your hands?"

"No. Inside."

"Ah." Bridget parked her truck to face the outside jumping arena at Briones Riding Academy. A woman DJ didn't know was taking her horse through the training jumps. "Annie is new since you have been gone. I am sure you will like her."

The horse in the arena ran out to the left on the first jump of the triple, and the woman cantered around to bring him straight back at the jump. He ran out again.

"What is she doing wrong?" Bridget asked DJ.

"She's distracted. She didn't bring him in straight."

"What else?"

"She dropped him on the takeoff, and she needs to keep him between her hands and legs. Might be using too much leg on the off side." How many times had she heard Bridget tell her those very same words?

"Now, how do you know that?"

"Repetition. You kept telling me."

"Did you conquer the bad habits?"

"Hope so."

"Did you get Herndon to keep from running out?"

"Most of the time. I have to remind myself to concentrate, to count, to do all the things right."

"Beating this new obstacle will take the same dedication you have always shown. This is a bump in the road, DJ, not an insurmountable chasm."

Some bump. It feels more like a mountain. Make that a range of mountains.

"I want you here starting next week. Your students are champing at the bit for you to return. I will give you one more class to teach until you are back to riding. When is Brad bringing Herndon back down?"

DJ shrugged. "Don't know."

"Do you want to stop in and see the kids?"

No, not the way I am.

"You do not have to, not today. But they really miss you. We all do."

"Can I go home now?"

"Yes. But Monday you will be here, correct?"

"I guess." DJ glanced up to catch a look—was it sorrow, pity, disgust?—that Bridget quickly erased from her face. "Thank you for bringing me."

"You are most welcome. I have three more little girls who want to learn to ride, and there is also a beginning jumping class. Which do you want?"

"By myself?"

"Why not?"

Why not? Why not? I can't saddle a horse or even brush one. . . . I can't—

Bridget stopped the truck in the turnaround in front of DJ's house. "I will see you. And, DJ, this, too, shall pass."

"Thanks. That's what everyone keeps telling me." DJ tried to open the door but couldn't get her fingers around the handle, so Bridget came around to open the door for her. *Right, "this will pass."*

DJ waved and watched Bridget drive off before limping up the walk. Her ankle ached with each step, so by the time she reached the door, all she could think of was lying down with her friend the ice pack. She stared at the door handle. No way was she going to ring the bell for help. She tried with one hand but couldn't cup it around the knob enough to turn it. She tried the other hand. No better.

Some names for the doorknob strutted through DJ's head. None of them were names her mother would approve of. She gritted her teeth. *So ring the bell, gimp, and get help. They tell you to ask for help.*

Instead, DJ cupped both hands around the handle and, squeezing them as tightly as she could, slowly twisted the knob until the door swung open. *Yes! At least I did something!* No sounds in the house. Her mother must be taking a nap, and Maria . . . who knew what Maria would be doing.

DJ limped up the stairs to her room, one foot up a step at a time, and finally collapsed on her bed. She propped her foot up on the pillows and closed her eyes. No way could she take the pain pills by herself, and no way could she get the ice packs. Too bad. Sleep was one thing she could do on her own, by herself.

"But, Gran, it's so hard." DJ clenched the phone between her ear and shoulder that evening before bed.

"I know, darlin', but you can't let this get you down. You're a fighter, and God's grace will get you through this."

A silence stretched. *I think Grace took a hike and hasn't come back yet.* But DJ knew better than to say that to her grandmother. Instead, she sighed. Sighing was fast becoming a habit.

"Have you been reading your Bible and praying?"

How DJ wished she could lie and say yes. But she didn't say anything. Gran would know.

"Ah, I see. Hard to turn the pages, isn't it?"

If she wanted to think that, so be it. But true, all pages were hard to turn.

Gran took in a deep breath. "Okay, this is what we do."

DJ could hear pages flipping.

"I will read, and then you will repeat after me, okay?"

" 'Kay."

" 'You have not because you do not ask . . . Ask for whatever you wish, and it will be done for you.' "

DJ's mind played with the words. " 'You do not have, because you do not ask.' " *Have I been asking?*

"Have you been asking?"

"Asking for what?"

"Well, what do you need the most right now?"

"My fingers to bend and hold things."

"What else?"

Another silence.

Gran read the verse again. "Now repeat after me." She read it again, phrase by phrase, and DJ echoed her.

"Now, I want you to think on these things as you go to sleep tonight. Will you do that?"

"I'll try." Oops. Bridget would get her for that. "I . . . I mean yes, I will."

And she did. Thinking on those words brought up other thoughts, along with tears, as DJ sobbed herself to sleep. That night there were no nightmares.

The next afternoon, after a morning of schoolwork, exercises, and frustration, DJ woke from her nap to hear the twins coming down the hall.

"Shh, DJ's sick."

"She's sleeping."

DJ threw back her covers and sat up. "No, she's not. DJ needs a hug—er, two hugs."

Giggles preceded two round faces with dancing blue eyes and wide grins. The boys threw themselves on her bed and snuggled next to her with their arms around her and hers around them. Queenie yipped and danced her way right into the middle, ecstatic at having three faces to lick all so close together.

"So how was school?"

"Arthur threw up at lunch—"

"And he had to go home." One finished the sentence for the other.

"Checkers the hamster got loose."

"Did you catch him?"

"No, Andrew did. He almost stepped on Checkers." Both boys shuddered.

"I got a blue balloon 'cause I was quiet." Bobby dug in his pocket to show her.

DJ knew this was a major accomplishment. Bobby had a hard time sitting still for long. "Good job! Do you think you can saddle General so you can have riding lessons?"

Lindy appeared in the doorway. "I was wondering what happened to the Bs."

"DJ's gonna give us a riding lesson." They bailed off the bed and ran to give Lindy strangle hugs.

"If you can cinch the saddle tight enough."

"Good. We'll do it all together." The smiling look Lindy sent her daughter said more than five minutes of talking could have. "You boys change your clothes while I get snacks ready. Then it's off to the horse we go."

The boys charged out of the room, shouting down the hall with Queenie adding to the din.

"If only we could bottle that energy, Robert would never have to work again." Lindy leaned against the doorjamb. "Need any help?"

"You could wrap my foot tighter."

Lindy did as asked. "How's that?"

"Better, since I'm gonna be walking on it."

"I'll take out a chair so you can sit while they ride." Lindy stroked DJ's head and down her shoulder. "Welcome back."

"M-o-m." But DJ didn't put the full twist on the word. She knew her mother was right; she was starting to feel like her old self again.

After they ate peanut butter and jelly sandwiches, the boys ran ahead to get General from the pasture and snap a lead around his neck to bring him up to the barn. While DJ watched, they groomed him and tacked him up.

As usual, he puffed up his belly when they tightened the girth. So Bobby led him around, and when they came back, Lindy tightened the girth by two notches.

"Billy rides first today." Lindy sank into one of the chairs she'd set up in the shade of the barn.

"How do you remember that stuff?" DJ stood by as Billy used the mounting block Robert had built and swung aboard.

"Checked the calendar." Lindy ran her fingers through her hair and let it fall back into place.

DJ smiled and watched to see Billy pick up the reins,

settle himself into the saddle, and squeeze his legs to signal General forward. "Very good."

"I think we need to be looking for another horse pretty soon so they each have one."

DJ stopped in the act of sitting down and stared at her mother. "Huh?"

"You heard me."

"I might have heard you, but I can't believe you really said it." DJ watched Billy walk General around the circle that had been worn into the short pasture grass. "Keep your back straight and heels down."

He did as she said.

"Okay, now trot when you come by us."

General shook his head but did as the boy signaled.

"He is so good with them." Lindy rubbed the back of DJ's neck.

"Mmm, that feels good. Has GJ had them cantering yet?"

"Some."

"I like to canter." Bobby leaned against his mother's knee.

"Okay, Billy, keep your hands together and low."

By the end of the lesson, both boys had walked, trotted, cantered, reversed, and trotted a figure eight.

"Boy, you two have come a long way. I am really proud of you." She rested her hands on their shoulders as they walked up to the deck. Billy turned his face and kissed her gloved fingers. The action was so swift she might have missed it had she not been watching. *God, please keep me from pulling back from my family and friends. Thanks for these two and my mom and dads. Thanks that I can walk, sorta.* She inhaled the scented air and let her shoulders relax on the exhale. *Just thanks.*

The boys bubbled like fountains at the dinner table until Robert finally made a referee's T with his hands for a time-out. "I think you talked my ears off." He clapped his hands over his ears. "They're gone! I can't find them."

"D-a-d-d-y," they said together, as usual.

DJ grinned at Robert's antics and the looks on the boys' faces.

As the boys and Maria cleared the table, Robert rose and came around to sit by DJ. "Welcome back, daughter. In spite of the short hair, you look and sound more like you than . . . than . . ." He raised his hands and dropped them. "Well, you know."

"I think I feel more like me, too. Did mom tell you what happened?"

"Only that you went somewhere with Bridget yesterday and today you gave the boys riding lessons—which, by the way, they had much been missing. Joe tried."

"He did a good job with them. They're learning fast. Did Mom tell you anything else?"

Robert rested his arms on the table and turned his head to watch her. "Like what?"

"About my blowing up at Debra Allendra yesterday."

"She mentioned it."

"I figured I was about due to be grounded after that."

"Well, at least you didn't break anything, and I have a feeling Debra has heard far worse. The important thing is that you look and sound better today. If a blowup was needed, I'm glad it's over."

"I . . ." DJ shivered. "I don't want to be like that."

"I know." Robert turned and took her hands in his to bend her fingers in. "You're doing better here, can you tell?"

"Not really. But now I push the backs of the fingers from one hand into the palm of the other. That way I can work 'em myself when I'm studying or whatever." She told him about the classes Bridget wanted her to teach. Dusk drifted down through the oak leaves. The hummingbirds drank their fill and headed off to bed. Two doves cooed up in the oak tree.

"So when are you going to start riding again?" Robert asked.

"How can I?"

"Well, you get on a horse and . . ."

"D-a-d." Now she sounded almost like the twins.

"Seriously. What's stopping you?"

DJ thought a moment. *What if I fall off . . . or hurt my hands worse? Be honest—you know the reason.* The voices ran after each other in her head, making her feel as if she were on a merry-go-round at warp speed.

"I . . . I'm scared." The whisper hurt not only her throat but her soul.

Robert folded his hands over hers. "Then let's figure out a way to do this so you won't be scared." He tipped her chin up with one finger so she had to look in his eyes. "And, Deej, I don't blame you one bit. I'd be scared, too, and probably not brave enough to admit it."

"Really?"

"Really."

But she woke in the middle of the night certain that she had been screaming again—and falling through the air. What would it take to get back on a horse?

11

"PLEASE, DJ, I really want you to."

DJ stared at her cousin, who right now closely resembled a dark-eyed puppy begging for treats. "Shawna . . ." *I can't tell her how scared I am. She'll think I'm a loser. Why not ride Major? He would never dump me—intentionally, that is.* DJ tried again. "He's your horse now."

"Sure, but he's still your friend. And he'll walk real gentle so you can get your balance back and everything. Joe will be there, too. Come on, DJ. Major is the perfect solution."

"Let me think about it."

"Now you sound like Gran." Shawna's dark eyes sparkled. "Since you use your left foot in the stirrup, you should be able to get on all right with the mounting block. I can bring him over here in two minutes. Please, DJ, let me do this."

DJ rolled her eyes and shook her head. "All right. Quit bugging me." But she smiled so that Shawna might think she didn't mean it. *How come everyone thinks they know what's best for me? Why can't they just leave me alone?*

Sure, like you were before? Her little voice got on the nagging wagon, not that it had ever been very quiet. DJ had just practiced ignoring the constant haranguing.

"Like right now?" Shawna was halfway to the door.

"I guess. But don't hurry so much that you make a mistake or something—like fall down the stairs."

"No, I leave that job for my big cousin." Shawna's giggle echoed back to DJ's room.

But I can't ride. I can't get my boot over my ankle yet.

Use your sandals with the true heel. You won't be jumping or anything.

"Just be quiet, can't you?" DJ rubbed her forehead, hoping that might still the argument going on in her mind. She looked down at her clothes. "I can't ride in this dress. Why didn't I think this through more?"

Queenie whimpered from her place on the bed. Her tail swept a couple of sheets of notebook paper to the floor. Since the therapist had given DJ orders to pick things up with her fingers, she bent down to do just that. The papers skidded away. Her fingers absolutely refused to meet with the paper in between. Finally she used both hands and scooped the papers up.

When she tried to open the drawers to get out her shorts and a T-shirt, she growled in frustration. "I hate this!"

"DJ, what is it?"

She could tell her mother was standing at the bottom of the stairs. "Just trying to use these useless hands of mine, that's all." DJ leaned her head against the wall and took in a deep breath.

"You want some help?"

"I guess." DJ glared at the drawers without handles. If only she could get rid of the cumbersome Jobst gloves. She tried again to insert her fingers under the lower edge of the drawer and pull out. She finally got her little finger under the rim and was able to open the drawer.

"What do you need?" Lindy crossed the room to stand by her daughter.

"My shorts and a T-shirt." She dug in the drawer for a

pair of drawstring shorts. Surely they would be easier to get on than her cutoffs.

"Really?"

DJ sighed as she used both hands to place the shorts, then the T-shirt, on the bed. "I'm going to ride Major."

"Now?" The smile nearly cracked Lindy's face.

"As soon as Shawna gets back here. She and Joe got this brilliant idea, and she wouldn't back off."

"Bless her little heart. She's wanted to help so badly."

"But I can't get my boot on over my ankle, so I guess I'll wear those sandals." DJ went to her closet and managed to snag the sandal straps and carry her shoes to the bed. "Can you please help me get dressed?"

"I'd be glad to."

"Bridget would have a horse if she saw me in these clothes."

"Bridget would be so thrilled you were riding that she wouldn't even notice." As they talked, Lindy pulled DJ's shorts up for her and tied the drawstring. "You have lost a lot of weight." She pulled the T-shirt over her daughter's head.

"It was all muscle, too." DJ slid her feet into the sandals so her mother could buckle them. "I feel like a baby. Mommy, dress me. Mommy, wash my hair. Mommy . . ."

"Mommy tickle you if you don't knock it off." Lindy swatted her on the rear. "I hear Joe's truck."

By the time DJ made it to the barn, Shawna rode in on Major and dismounted at the gate.

"Now, this is one happy day," Joe said, opening the gate for Shawna to walk Major through. He patted DJ on the shoulder. "You're looking good, kid. We'll get some sun back on your face and you'll look even better. Here, I brought this for you." He handed DJ her helmet.

"Thanks. You think of everything." DJ took the helmet in both hands and set it on her head. "Now if you'll buckle the strap." She looked into her grandfather's eyes as he squinted to get the buckle adjusted. *What a kind and wonderful man you are.* "You know what, GJ?"

"No, what?"

"I sure do love you a whole lot." She had to swallow after she said it as the tears immediately clogged her throat.

Joe put his arms around her and hugged her close. "Well, let me tell you, the feeling is sure mutual, darlin'. Now, you just get yourself up on that horse, and we can all know better that the healing is really happening."

DJ stood in front of Major and let him wuffle her hair, in her ear, and down to her hands, where he nosed her gloves, then her pocket for a carrot. "At least I can pet you now, you old sweetie, even if these gloves are strange to you." She stroked down his cheeks and up around his ears, inhaling deeply at the same time. "Ah, Major, you smell so good." DJ closed her eyes in delight. "I didn't realize how much I missed my friend here. Thanks, Shawna."

"For being a pain?" Shawna flipped up the saddle skirt. "What hole do you want the stirrups on?" She buckled the leathers into place and did the other side. "Okay, he's ready."

"Me too, I guess." DJ swallowed the butterflies and, using Joe's arm to steady her, climbed the three steps to the top of the mounting block. Shawna led Major to stand in the right place so DJ could slide her injured foot across his back. Then with Joe reaching up to steady her, DJ settled into the saddle. She found the stirrups with her toes, let out a deep breath, and relaxed in the saddle.

Major turned his head to sniff at her toes, then shook his head.

"My feet do not stink. If it's just because I don't have boots on, too bad." DJ could feel the base of her foot on the metal stirrup. She eyed the reins.

"How about if Shawna leads him and I walk beside you?" Joe laid a hand on her knee. "That way you can concentrate on your balance right now and worry about managing the reins later."

DJ swallowed a determined butterfly and nodded. "Let's go."

General nickered from his stall, where Joe had put him so Major wouldn't be distracted.

DJ laid her hands on her thighs and told herself to relax. *Come on, body, we can do this.*

"Do you feel light-headed?" Joe asked as they walked across the pasture.

"No. Just strange to be sitting here and not using the reins." She flexed her feet, pushing her heels down, then stood in the stirrups. She could feel Joe's concern, and Shawna looked over her shoulder to make sure everything was all right.

"Come on, guys, no worrying allowed." DJ settled back in the saddle. How good it felt! She tipped her face so the sun shone on it. With her eyes closed she let the motion seep into every cell of her body. A step at a time, once around the one-acre pasture. Moment by moment, DJ felt strength and energy flooding into her body. They stopped at the mounting block, where Lindy stood leaning on the upper aluminum rail.

"I don't need to ask how you're doing. Your face is glowing like you're lit from the inside. If the sun went behind a cloud, we'd all still feel warm."

"Thanks, all of you, for pushing me to do this." DJ leaned forward and wrapped her arms around Major's neck. "I was scared I would feel dizzy and fall off."

"We wouldn't have let you fall off. Even if you couldn't do more than just sit with Major standing still, it was time for you to get back on the horse."

"Shawna, I think I'd like to try holding the reins and see how my hands do."

"Good."

DJ stared at the large strap of leather. She slid her fingers under it, palms up.

"Does it hurt?" Shawna asked, her brow wrinkling in concern.

"No. I feel the pressure, but not enough to hurt." DJ closed her hands as much as she was able to in order to keep the reins from sliding off. "So much for keeping my reins even, huh?"

"I'd say just keeping the reins is pretty good." Lindy rubbed her bulging belly. "With my luck, this little one is saying, 'Get me on that horse.' "

"You want to ride, Mom?" DJ said with a grin. "Shawna and Joe could lead you around."

"Thanks, but no thanks. Seven months pregnant is not a good time to start horseback riding. However, later . . ." She shrugged. "We'll see."

"Let's go again," DJ said to Shawna. This time DJ made sure her posture was straight; she kept her attention looking ahead and was totally aware of the reins in her cupped hands. When she tried turning her hands over, the rein slid loose.

"Joe, could you help me, please?"

"Sure 'nough."

He redid the reins, and DJ squeezed her legs to signal Major forward. At least part of her worked right. Of course, Major was such a sweetie and so well trained that she could probably ride him without reins, just using her legs and shifting her weight. She cupped one hand over the other to hold the reins. Now, if she'd been riding Western, where the reins were held together in one hand, this might have been easier.

"Shawna, you want to try a real slow trot?"

"Sure. Come on, Major."

DJ squeezed her legs and picked up the post as though she'd never been away. When Shawna began to huff and puff, they went back to walking. Major pulled at the bit just enough to let DJ know that he would like to keep going.

When they returned to the mounting block, DJ leaned forward and hugged her old friend again. She pressed with her outer leg to get him closer to the block, then laid the rein back on his neck. Placing her left foot on the block, she swung her right leg back over his rump and stood upright. *I did it! Thank you, God. I rode again.*

"You want to go again tomorrow?" Shawna had remounted Major, ready to ride him back to Joe's pasture, where he was stabled.

"Yeah, I do. Gotta work these hands more so I can hold the reins." She clenched and straightened her fingers. "The day I can hold a pencil, I should be able to hold the reins."

"What if we glued foam rubber to the reins like we have with your eating utensils?" Joe ran his fingers along the leather strap. "Don't see why it wouldn't work. You don't need strength with this old boy." He patted Major's shoulder. "Does she, old son?"

Major shook his head and rubbed his forehead against Joe's shoulder. The two of them had been through a lot in their years on the San Francisco mounted patrol, including more than one shooting. Major wore a scar on his shoulder to prove it.

"Shawna, do you mind if I ride Major while I'm recovering?" DJ braced her rear against the mounting block.

"No. I want you to ride him as much as you want. Anything that will help you get strong again."

"Thanks." DJ rubbed Major's nose and tickled his whiskery upper lip. He nibbled the ends of her fingers and licked her wrist. "Now, if only I had some carrots, huh? See, the problem is, I can't get things out of my pockets yet. Of course, I can't get anything *in* my pockets to take out again—yet." *Yet.* Such a small word but such huge meaning. No longer *if* but *yet*.

"That's right, DJ," Lindy said softly. "You've come a long way, and a lot of it in the last few days. Like the therapist has said so often, the rest of this is up to you. She glanced at her watch. "Oh my, I have to go get the boys." They were playing at a school friend's house a couple of miles away. "Maria has snacks ready to set out if you want to tie Major up and stay awhile, Shawna."

"Okay." Shawna glanced at her grandfather. "If you want to, GJ."

They were still sitting on the deck laughing and enjoying the chocolate chip cookies when the boys burst through the house and threw themselves at their grandfather for hugs and then tore around the table to get the same from DJ. They snatched cookies off the plate, one in each hand and an extra for General, and skipped their way down to the barn.

"Did a whirlwind just blow through here?" Joe righted a chair that they'd knocked over.

DJ laughed around her mouthful of cookie. She made her fingers grip the glass of lemonade and took a sip. How good it felt to be able to eat and drink on her own at last.

"So how difficult will it be to glue foam rubber on the reins?"

"Not at all. I have both glue and foam at home. We'll use an old pair of reins. I was thinking that if the glue didn't work, I'd take them down to the shoe repair place to have him sew them on. You'll have them by tomorrow. Maybe we could try them out after church."

"You're the best."

"Do you want to keep Major here for a while, then?" Shawna reached for another cookie. "He could use that other stall again. I can ride here just as well as at GJ and Gran's."

"I . . . I guess."

"Do you good to muck out a stall for a change." Joe

slapped his hands on the table. "Well, I've got to get back home. Mel has a list a mile long for me to do." He shook his head. "I don't know where she gets all her ideas. You'd think with being so busy with her illustrations, she wouldn't have time to think of new stuff for the yard and the house."

"What are you working on now?" DJ asked.

"Oh, she wants a ladder over the top of the garage door so she can plant a wisteria or something to cross it. Some picture Mel saw looked real pretty, so we're going to have one."

"Poor GJ." DJ and Shawna said the words at the same time. But when they went to slap high fives, Shawna pulled back.

"Hey, you can't hurt me that easy." DJ held her hands up and Shawna slapped with the lightest touch.

When Joe headed for his truck, the two girls made their way to the barn, where Major waited, drowsing with one hind foot cocked. Shawna untied the lead shank and led him out of the gate. DJ patted him again and walked them out to the driveway.

Since she'd given the boys their riding lessons in the morning, she went back to the kitchen for the ice packs and then upstairs to build a pillow tower and collapse on her bed with her iced foot high in the air.

"I rode again. Thank you, Jesus. I rode again. And I wasn't dizzy." She studied her foot. "There must be a way to get my chore boots on at least."

Sandals weren't allowed around the rings and barns at Briones. What had Bridget been thinking when she insisted DJ be there for a class on Monday? She heard the phone ringing downstairs but fell asleep before she thought much about it.

12

ON MONDAY DJ HAD TO CALL Bridget and cancel teaching her new class because the therapist had changed her appointment. DJ grumped out to the car and sulked against the door.

"I'm sorry, DJ, but therapy is the most important part of your life right now." Lindy glanced away from her driving to give her daughter a stern look. "And schoolwork is second. The Academy has to come third or wherever." She stopped at a light and glanced at her daughter again.

DJ could feel her mother studying her, but she refused to look up, staring at her hands instead. *I finally get to do something I want again, and someone messes it up.* "It's just not fair."

"No, it's not fair, but then, no one said life is fair."

"That's Gran's line."

"I know. I stole it. But I sure remember hating it when she told it to me when I was your age."

"So why say it to me?"

"Because it's true and fits right now. Have you been working your hands today?"

"Of course. What do you think I do all the time?" DJ knew she was being a smart mouth, but the words flew out before she thought them through.

"Well, you haven't been doing them here in the car."

DJ flexed her fingers and used one hand to push in the fingers of the other. She'd forgotten to bring the rubber-coated bag of tiny beads that Gran had found at the pharmacy. She now had one in bright pink and another in purple. While they were ideal for squeezing, DJ still spent time bending her fingers in with as much force as she was able.

DJ thought back to Sunday afternoon. Brad and Jackie had driven down from Santa Rosa for a barbecue, and with all the family there, it seemed like old times. At least no one had to feed her anymore. Brad had asked her when she wanted him to bring Herndon down.

The thought of riding Herndon with her hands not working any better gave her goose bumps. He could take off so easily, and how would she stop him?

"I won't be jumping him for a while." She could hear herself all over again, saying words that made her feel like the sun forgot to come out. Two months had passed since the fire, and DJ still wasn't sure she could handle Herndon.

But the reins that Joe fixed for her had sort of worked, and she'd ridden Major by herself. But then, he responded to leg signals as much as rein. And *he* would never run away with her. . . .

"We're here."

DJ looked up to see the medical center ahead of them. She'd totally lost track of time. That happened more often than she liked to think—or admit.

"Get that grumpy look off your face. It doesn't become you." Lindy reached back in the minivan for her purse, groaning as she stretched over the seat. "This belly gets in the way of everything."

But at least it won't be long until you are back to normal. DJ wisely kept the thought to herself as she lagged behind her mother going into the physical therapy unit.

"So how're you doing?" Jody asked.

"I rode Major the last two days—yesterday by myself. We glued foam rubber to the reins."

"Wonderful. How'd the ankle do?"

"Hurt when I tried getting into my chore boots, but . . ." DJ shook her head and shrugged. "Just hurt too bad."

"Your ankle should be back to normal in a few more days. Just be patient."

"I know." While they were talking, Jody worked with DJ's hands. She removed the gloves and worked them that way, examining the red skin and scars, then put the gloves back on and taught DJ several new exercises. "Be creative in finding ways to do things on your own, but don't push yourself to the point of total frustration. Like the reins. That's a good idea, but if the horse ran away . . ."

"Major won't, but Herndon, my jumper, isn't so dependable."

"And your balance was okay? No dizziness?"

"None." At the smile that lit up Jody's face, DJ knew that was good news. "But I haven't tried jumping yet."

Jody smiled again and raised one eyebrow. She turned to Lindy. "I think the DJ I heard about is coming back. Good for you, girl."

DJ nodded her thanks. "I'm trying."

"Knock 'em dead, kid. See you on Thursday, regular time."

"How . . . how much longer do I have to keep coming?" DJ didn't look at her mother as she asked the question.

"Until we can no longer do anything for you. We want you to have full mobility again, so you'll have to keep coming back for a while. I know that as you get back to normal, coming will seem like a waste of time, but humor me, okay?"

"I guess."

Amy was waiting at the house when DJ got home. "I got a whole new bunch of orders from the business club at school. They are so pumped about our cards. Sure wish you had been there, too."

"Me too."

"When we fill these, we'll be out of cards again."

"That many?" DJ thought of all the packets in the drawers and shelves in her room. She looked at her hands. There was no way she could count, package, and seal cards yet.

"That's wonderful," Lindy said as she walked in behind them. "Maybe it's time we found a place to package them. I've checked with an organization for mentally challenged adults, and they can take on simple jobs like this. I know it will bring down the profit level, but there's only so much you can do."

"Then we'd be helping someone else, too," Amy said.

Leave it to Amy. DJ wished she'd thought of that. All she could think of was not being able to draw or package or even . . . Well, she could at least help pack the cartons for shipping.

"So what do you think, DJ?"

"Whatever. Sounds fine with me. If we think it costs too much, we can go back to doing it ourselves when . . ." She raised her hands, which spoke for themselves.

"Well, I gotta get over to the barns. We'll have to pack those tonight."

"Yeah, but maybe Mom and I can get it done." DJ looked to her mother, who nodded. *Then at least I'll feel like I'm doing something.* She thought of her homework; the pile seemed to grow every time she left the room. "Say hi to everyone for me."

"I will." Amy headed for her bicycle and on out the driveway.

Lindy looked at the order sheets Amy had left. "Now?"

"I guess." DJ counted packets and packed the boxes, feeling like she had fifteen thumbs. But she got it done while her mother checked off the order sheets and made out the shipping labels. DJ tried taping the boxes, but the tape stuck everywhere except where she wanted it to—the thought of kicking the box clear across the room held great possibilities. "Could you please finish this?" Asking for help hadn't gotten any easier.

"Sure. Hey, we did that pretty fast." Lindy took the tape gun and had the six boxes sealed in minutes. "Let's run these to UPS right now before it closes."

"Ten minutes?"

"We can make it."

DJ held out her arms, and Lindy stacked four of the boxes under DJ's chin and carried the other two herself. She snagged her purse off the table by the door and away they went, calling their destination to Maria as they hurried to the car.

They made it just as the woman was closing the door, but she was nice enough to let them in.

"Sorry we're so late." Lindy put her boxes on the counter. "Oh, we forgot your checkbook."

"No, I brought it." DJ pulled it from her pocket and held it up. The woman behind the counter had no idea what a feat that was, but Lindy patted her daughter's cheek.

"Good girl. That deserves a celebration milk shake on the way home."

The jamoca almond fudge malt tasted mighty good.

DJ rode Major again Tuesday morning after mucking out his stall. Holding the grooming brushes was easier than she thought it would be, and the sheer pleasure of brushing a horse again made her whistle a tune. She'd even gotten an hour in on her homework before the tutor arrived.

Being able to take oral tests instead of written made her day even sunnier.

"Good job," Debra said. "We'll plan on midterms next Wednesday. How's that?"

"Do we have to?" DJ groaned. Tests to study for already?

"We can wait a week if we have to, but let's get them done before we should be doing quarter finals. I'm hoping you'll be able to go back to school in the next few weeks, at least part time."

Just because she'd been up early the last couple of days to take care of Major didn't mean she wanted to go back to school. Holding a grooming brush was a hundred times easier than a pen or pencil.

That afternoon DJ and Gran got caught in a traffic jam on their way back from therapy. While DJ called Bridget on the cell phone to say she might not make it, she had a hard time throwing off the grumps. Gran patted her knee. "Sorry, but these things happen."

"I know." *But why me?*

On Thursday DJ cantered Major around the pasture. While her mother had to hook and unhook the girth, DJ managed everything else. The October sun sparkled on the dew in the grass and highlighted a spider web on the fence.

Pushing her fingers closed had become such a habit, DJ was no longer aware she was doing it. Whenever she sat down, she picked up the squeeze-me balls and kept working. If her ankle didn't still hurt at times, she'd have been out running.

But the ice packs were still part of her routine, and now, thanks to Gran's advice, she'd started rubbing vitamin E oil into her hands. Gran said it would help the scars heal faster.

Brad called on the last Wednesday in October. "So when can I bring Herndon back down for you?"

DJ swallowed before answering. "I . . . I don't think I'm ready for him yet. Bridget said I could ride Megs as soon as I can jump again." *I wish I trusted Herndon, but I don't. If he runs away with me, I don't think I can stop him.*

"How about I come get you next weekend, then, and you can visit him up here. Stormy's forgotten who you are, I think. I take pictures out there to show her, but all she wants is carrots."

DJ chuckled over the ache his words brought. Her little Arabian filly was growing up without her.

"Let me ask Mom, and I'll call you back."

"Okay. How is your mom?"

"She says she feels as big as a house, but I think she looks beautiful. I felt the baby kicking last night. Awesome."

"Okay, kiddo. We'll see you Saturday or Sunday, whichever works best for you. Jackie said to tell you she'll put the pasta on."

They said good-bye and DJ hung up the phone. Was she ready to ride Herndon? And could her hands be trusted to be even with the reins? No sense in teaching her horse bad habits.

Or are you just afraid? That voice again. Were her reasons just excuses?

"Your hands are looking good," Dr. Niguri said in her appointment on Friday back at the UC San Francisco Burn Center. He checked DJ's range of motion and nodded with a smile. "I can tell you have been working really hard. I was thinking we might need another skin graft, but now I don't think so." He traced a fingertip over the worst scars. "By this time next year these will be such fine lines, you will have to look hard to see them. It's a good thing you are young and healthy and have a great attitude—all strong marks in your favor."

DJ glanced at her mother, who gave a minishrug. "My attitude isn't always the best."

"You been down some?"

DJ nodded.

"Like way down, can't see the sky looking up?"

DJ nodded again. "All I wanted to do was sleep."

The doctor nodded and continued working her fingers. "Perfectly normal. I'd be more concerned if you were happy all the time. That would tell me you were covering up, and that's not good. More dangerous in the long run." He picked up the Jobst gloves and put them back on DJ's hands.

"When can I quit wearing these?"

"We'll start easing off, like a couple of hours at a time, in a month or so. Your hands could still swell up, and that would be a major step back. Don't be in a rush to get rid of them. They're doing you a big favor while all the muscles and tissue in your hands rebuild." He stood. "So I'll see you here in another month. How's the ankle doing?"

"Almost back to normal. But it aches when I've been on it too much."

"Well, pain is a good thing, you know."

DJ gave him a you've-got-to-be-crazy look.

"Now, think this through." He half-sat on the edge of his desk, arms clasped across the clipboard he held to his chest. "If that ankle didn't hurt, what would you be doing?"

"Walking more, running to get back in shape, riding more."

"Right, and keeping that sprain from healing correctly."

DJ sighed and nodded. He'd made his point. So now she had to be grateful for pain, too.

"The earlier you learn to listen to your body, the wiser and healthier you will become. Our bodies are designed to heal themselves in miraculous ways. When we get enough sleep, eat right, and keep from more damage, the healing happens. And in your case, I'm sure all the prayers have accelerated the healing process. I wish all my patients had the prayer power behind them that you have had."

"Yes, we've been incredibly blessed that way." Lindy used a tissue to wipe her nose and eyes. "We just can't thank you enough for all you've done for us."

"Glad I could help." He ushered them to the office door. "Uh, DJ, if I ever have a patient that I think would be helped by talking with you, would you be willing?"

"Sure. You want me to bring Major, too?"

"The horse?" The doctor threw back his head and laughed, the kind of laugh that made everyone around laugh with him. "Probably not, but that story is still going around the hospital. How Karen dared to take you out there is beyond me. But it turned out well, so . . ." He chuckled again. "Sure wish I had seen it all."

They said their good-byes and DJ followed her mother out to the parking lot. She'd hoped they could go see Karen, but it was her day off. They headed home across the Bay Bridge, which arched across the bay from San Francisco to Buena Vista Island, and then on to Oakland. A huge cargo ship poked its prow out from passing under the bridge as they drove over. Thanks to their new higher-riding van, DJ could see the many ships and boats in the water below. A haze hung over the bay, blurring the edges of the cargo-loading cranes in the Oakland port and the skyline of San Francisco behind them.

"So what are you planning for this afternoon?" Lindy asked as she changed lanes.

"Teaching the jumping class at the Academy. Then riding Megs."

"Are you ready for that?"

"Hope so. I can't see her running away with me."

DJ had fun starting out the two ladies who wanted to learn to jump and were on riding school horses. She had them walking, then trotting, over the cavalletti just like Bridget had started DJ so long ago. They had to count the strides, and when she finally let them take the first jump, one of them laughed out loud with joy. DJ knew she was going to like the woman.

By the end of class, the horses were sweating, the riders were sweating, and DJ wished she were. While she liked teaching, this standing in one place rather than jumping herself was the pits.

"So you going to ride today?" Tony Andrada waited by the gate for her class to end.

"How'd you know that?" DJ waved her pupils off and held the gate for Tony to ride through.

"Word gets around. We sure miss you around here."

"We'll, I'm back, sorta. And yes, Bridget wants me to try Megs today and see how we do."

"Jumping?"

DJ shrugged. "Probably not the first day I ride her. Knowing Bridget, I'm going to be doing a lot of dressage to get back in shape."

She didn't admit that the thought of jumping sent her resident butterflies into total panic.

13

"MORE LEG, LEFT LEG."

DJ did as ordered, but after forty-five minutes on basic dressage drills, she felt limper than cooked spaghetti. If she focused on keeping her reins in anything close to a normal position, her legs turned flabby or her shoulders rounded or . . . there was always another *or*.

"All right, DJ, that is enough for the first time." Bridget crossed the arena to stand at Megs' shoulder and laid a hand on DJ's knee. "You must not try so hard. You are wearing yourself out with the tension."

"But . . ." DJ closed her eyes for a second, sucked in a deep breath, and let it all out. Her whole body sighed. "I am such a mess."

"No, you are recovering, and that will take time. Poor Megs was only confused a time or two. You know that you mainly guide her with your legs anyway, so do not worry so much about what your hands are doing."

"Or *not* doing." DJ's jaw ached because she had been clamping her teeth to keep her focus. Her mind still had a tendency to go off and play somewhere else, no matter what she ordered it to do. It was nearly November, and here she was sweating like it was July. And not from the heat.

Her hands hurt, too. Even with the foam rubber on the

reins, they dug into her tender flesh. Maybe she had been gripping them too hard.

"I think you should not ride Megs every day. Then when you ride Major you can just enjoy yourself. You may do some of the drills, but only to refresh his memory. Not for perfection."

There goes that idea. DJ realized her mind had gone into high-speed planning to ride hours each day to gain her skill back. "All right, if you think so." She almost said *but* before grabbing the word back. *But* could be termed argumentative, and Bridget didn't tolerate arguments.

"Thanks, Bridget, for loaning me Megs again." She patted the mare's shoulder. "You came out of retirement for me. Thanks, old girl." Megs pulled at the bit, getting impatient with standing still.

Back in the barn DJ asked one of the other student workers to unbuckle the girth and throat latch so she could remove the tack. At least she could grasp big things now, like a saddle.

The twins followed DJ as she made her way upstairs to her room.

"Do you hurt, DJ?"

"Want some ice cream? Maria's got Popsicles. You want one?"

"Mommy's taking a nap."

"You gonna take a nap?"

"When can we ride General?"

DJ tried to sort out their questions. "Yes, my hands hurt. Yes, I'd like a Popsicle. How about you ride General after dinner?" She let herself flop back on the bed, only to get a wet doggy kiss.

The boys ran off to fetch the Popsicle.

But when the banana-flavored treat came, DJ realized she would have done better with ice cream. At least that she could eat with a spoon. She groaned and shook her head. "Fiddle. Double fiddle."

The boys stared at her, each with a long Popsicle in his mouth, eyes round above it.

Maria appeared at the door. "I bring you ice cream. Popsicle not good with sore hands."

DJ willingly surrendered the Popsicle and, taking the fat-handled spoon, dug in to Tin Parlor ice cream.

Before she left, Maria arranged the pillows and laid the ice packs nearby for DJ's hands. "You okay now?"

"Yes, thank you. I didn't think when I asked for a Popsicle." DJ licked the fudge sauce from her spoon.

"Good. Come, boys. DJ looks like she needs to sleep."

Halloween arrived without DJ donning a costume to answer the door for trick-or-treaters. After about the fourth group, Lindy took over because opening the door was starting to hurt DJ's hands. Robert took the boys—one dressed as a cowboy, the other as an Indian, thanks to Gran's creative sewing—to a party at school.

When the horde subsided, DJ and her mother crashed at either end of the long sofa in the family room.

"Would you unwrap this for me, please?" DJ handed her mother the Snickers bar she'd hoarded from the goody bowl.

Lindy obliged and took another sip from her pink lemonade. "That's one way to stay out of the candy, not being able to open the things." She reached for another baby carrot. The doctor had said that she needed to slow down her weight gain or the baby would be as big as a toddler before birth.

"Do you have time to read my manuscript one of these days?" Lindy waved her carrot in the air. "I need some suggestions."

"Sure. Don't see how I could help, though. Gran would be better."

"Oh, she's reading it, too. I just don't want it to sound too . . . too . . ." Lindy crunched her carrot. "Too stuffy, too scholarly. I think it sounds like it was written by an MBA."

"But that's what you are."

"I know, but it needs to read easier, I think—be more interesting."

"Whatever."

"As soon as I get it back from Gran, I'll give it to you." Lindy stared at her daughter, her mind obviously running somewhere else. "No, I'll print you out a fresh copy. But not tonight." She smoothed her hands over her beach-ball belly. "This one's been busy today. Must be redecorating in there."

DJ smiled at her mother's description. One day she'd been sure there were two and they were having a wrestling match. "What did the ultrasound show when you went today?"

"Everything looks good. They're still not positive it's a girl—this little busybody keeps turning away from the camera. Never thought I'd have a camera-shy kid before it was born. The one technician is sure it's a girl, though."

"A baby sister. Wow!"

"But there's still a possibility it's a boy."

"Already got two of them."

"I'm just praying for a healthy baby. Boy, girl . . . the yellow trim and Noah's ark work for either." They'd finished decorating the baby's room the week before, so all was ready.

Lindy rubbed her belly. "Six weeks to go, and if I remember right, these seem the longest."

"The baby will be healthy. You've done all the right things."

"Just pray, too, okay?"

DJ nodded. It wasn't too long ago that her mother would not have mentioned praying or God's will. She'd figured to leave all the praying up to Gran, who was a master at it. Robert had helped her change into a praying mom.

DJ yawned and stretched. "I better see if I can get in an hour or two of studying before I hit the sack." She gave her mother a kiss, got one and a hug in return, and headed for the stairs.

Sunday after church, they all climbed in the Bronco and drove up to Gladstone Farms, Brad's ranch in Santa Rosa.

"Do we get to play with Stormy?"

"How big is she?"

DJ shrugged. "Not sure. I haven't seen her since August, and that was three months ago. Foals grow fast, you know."

"How fast?"

"Can we ride her?"

Sometimes DJ wished they didn't ask so many questions. "Nope. Can't ride her until she's at least two." What would it be like to ride a filly she helped raise? Stormy had been DJ's own horse since shortly after her birth. Showing her in halter had been a blast.

DJ looked at her hands. How long until she could show, whether halter, flat, dressage, or jumping? Bridget still had DJ on Megs two days a week riding dressage. No jumping until she could handle the reins better. But better didn't seem to be happening anywhere near fast enough.

They turned into the long, curving drive and kept to the right to go up to the house. Gladstone Farms, bordered by the river on the east side, lay around a center hill, where the house nestled amid ancient oaks and poplars; a tall red-wood reigned above the azaleas and Liquidambar. Leaves ranging from scarlet to burgundy to gold still clung to some of the trees.

Brad met them before they got out of the car. "Hi, all. Do you want to drive on down to the barn or walk?"

Lindy smiled at his greeting. "I know I should walk, but how about we drive down?"

"We can walk," the boys chorused.

"We'll all ride." Robert glanced at the boys in the rear-view mirror.

"Jackie and I will meet you down there, then." He tapped on the glass of DJ's back window and gave her a thumbs-up.

Down at the low white barns, which less than a year earlier had been half filled with water from the catastrophic spring flooding, they climbed out of the Bronco. Robert had to shush the boys, who were wound tighter than a tornado.

"You can run around out here, but in the barn you have to walk slow and not shout because you don't want to scare the horses."

"We'll be good" came the twin chorus.

Brad hugged DJ, then kept an arm over her shoulders as Jackie hugged her, too. Jackie held DJ at arm's length so she could make sure she was all right, then hugged her again.

"I am so glad and grateful to have you here," she whispered in DJ's ear. "That was far too close a call. How are your hands? The rest, I can see, is beautiful as ever."

DJ held up her gloved hands. "I have to keep these gloves on so I don't get any swelling. But I can almost touch my thumbs to my fingers now. See?" DJ focused on her right thumb and finger as slowly, slowly they drew closer together. She glanced up to catch the sheen of tears in Brad's eyes. "I'm okay, Dad. Or I will be. Not to worry."

"Easy for you to say." He drew her close to his side. "One

thing's sure, you look a lot better than you did two months ago." His shudder said it all. "Let's go see your friend. I told Herndon you were coming, and he put on his best suit." Letting go of her, he slid the barn door open. They stepped into an aisle that ran the length of the barn, with foaling stalls near the door and individual stalls farther down. Shavings covered the dirt floor, and brass nameplates glinted on the stall doors.

DJ whistled even though Herndon had most likely forgotten. But a whinny, not a nicker, let her know he heard—and remembered. His fine head reached out of the stall door, and he banged a hoof in impatience.

DJ felt her throat clog. "He remembers me."

"He's not such a snob anymore. I think that fire scared the snob right out of him," Jackie said.

"Did he get burned anywhere?"

"No, you got him out first before the fire spread too far. He fared better than some of the other horses, but they all lived thanks to you and your quick thinking."

DJ stopped in front of Herndon and let him snuffle her arms, face, and hands before he nudged her chest. "Yeah, big man, I brought you treats." DJ fumbled in her sweat shirt pouch and brought out a horse cookie—Herndon's favorite. He took it from her palm and, even while munching, leaned into her fingers as they stroked his cheek, his ears, and down his long neck.

When Brad opened the stall door so she could go in, Herndon moved over but not away. He even lowered his head so she could reach more easily.

"He's never been like this before."

"I know. I told you, we have a different horse here than we did before." Jackie joined them in the stall. "After he calmed down—for a while any noise startled him—he let this mellow side show. I've been riding him so he doesn't get rusty, and he's pure pleasure to ride now. You want to try him?"

DJ held up her hands. "I still have to use the foam rubber on the reins and can't grip tight enough, so I guess not."

"You think we'd let something like that stop you?" Brad showed her the fat reins on Herndon's bridle. "Jackie has ridden him with the new bit so he won't be surprised. You don't have to, but . . ."

How could she say no? DJ swallowed the butterflies that had suddenly woken up and started their aerial show.

What if he runs away with me? Can I stop him? DJ hoped her fear didn't show on her face. But Herndon would sense it anyway.

"How about we put him on a lunge line for you. That way you can get the feel of him again without having to worry about controlling him." Jackie took the bridle off the hook and set about tacking him up.

"Yes, please." *Now, why didn't you think of that?* DJ had hoped her resident nag had stayed home. No such luck. "I'll have to use a mounting block. Can't pull myself up yet."

"No problem. There's one in the arena. You want to ride inside or out?" Brad handed Jackie the saddle.

"Inside, I guess."

"You got a horse for us to ride?" Bobby or Billy asked.

"Shh." Lindy reminded them that the question wasn't polite.

"Sure do, but she's bigger than your General."

"That's okay." But when the boys started to jump, Robert laid a heavy hand on each of their shoulders.

"How about we let DJ ride first, and then we'll saddle up the old girl for you," Brad suggested.

"What's her name?" chimed the Bs.

"We call her Queenie because she's been around the longest."

"Like our dog! Is she black-and-white?"

"Nope, dapple-gray."

While they chattered, DJ felt her shoulders tense, along with the muscles down her back. Herndon was acting like her long-lost friend right now, but he might switch personalities and go back to who he used to be right quick.

"You ready?"

"I guess." DJ knew her reply was barely lukewarm, but it was all she could manage at the moment. *Oh, God, please don't let me fall off.*

14

RIDING HERNDON WAS LIKE FLOATING on a cloud.

"He feels good, doesn't he?" Jackie kept turning with the lunge line, watching DJ and grinning as if she'd just won the lottery.

"He sure does." Gone was that tight, I'm-about-to-explode feeling she'd always had with him before. He walked flat out, loose and relaxed. After several circuits, at DJ's signal he picked up an easy trot. DJ posted with scarcely any effort. When she fumbled with the reins, he flicked his ears back and forth but kept an even stride.

"You did just fine," Jackie said when DJ slowed Herndon to a walk and turned him in to the center of the ring.

"Thanks to a lot of hours already on Major and Megs. Bridget hasn't let me jump yet. Got to get better hands first."

"They'll come. And you know he's ready whenever you are. I figured the only way you'd see the difference in him is by riding him yourself. He's faced the worst thing that could happen and survived, and now he's relaxed."

"Have you jumped him?" DJ leaned forward and stroked Herndon's barely sweat-darkened neck.

"A bit, and you can tell he loves it. I've been doing mostly dressage to keep him in condition. You sure look good on him. I can't wait to see you in the ring again."

"Mmm."

"You don't sound too sure."

"Just taking one day at a time."

Brad strolled into the arena, leading the gray mare with both boys astride. They waved at DJ and said something to Brad that made him laugh. Robert and Lindy came in behind them.

"You want to go some more? We can take up more of the line."

Sure. Or can I ride him by myself . . . or not. DJ couldn't make up her mind. She wanted to—oh, how she wanted to—but . . . "No, let's put him away so the boys can ride without any interference. Guess I just don't want to take any chances . . . yet."

Jackie smiled up at her. "Good enough. Then we'll get dinner on the table. All I have to do is cook the linguine. I tried a new recipe for clam sauce. Brad says it's the best ever." She led Herndon over to the mounting block, where DJ dismounted.

"Herndon, thanks for the easy ride. Soon we'll jump again. I promise." Herndon nosed her cheek and tipped his head toward her so she would rub the tip of his ear. As soon as Jackie had the tack off, DJ took the brushes and, using both hands, brushed him down.

"You do okay with those, huh?"

"Big stuff is fine, as long as I don't have to exert much pressure. But buckles, pencils, paper, narrow straps are all beyond me. I feel like a total klutz at times, but at least my balance is back and I move with the horse again. The first time I rode Major I felt like a stick."

DJ used both hands to pick up the cloth and wipe around Herndon's eyes and down his face. "There you go, big horse. Thanks again."

He nickered when they walked away. DJ turned back to

give him one more pat and hug. "Guess you really are mine now, aren't you, big horse?" She could feel tears working their way out. Would she ever get over crying so easily?

They stopped to give Matadorian, Brad's foremost stallion, a couple of pats, then ambled out to the pasture, where the last crop of foals grazed and played. As soon as they saw Jackie, they all came trotting up to the fence.

"Hey, Stormy, I almost didn't recognize you." DJ held out her hand to her filly, who sniffed it and went to Jackie for a treat. "I have a bit of horse cookie left in my pocket, if you could please get it out." She motioned to her pouch. "The piece is too small for me to pick up. I should have brought more."

Jackie did so, and DJ held out her hand with the bit of treat on her palm. Two of the youngsters came to inspect, but DJ pushed off the other one and let Stormy have it. The filly munched happily, nodding her approval.

"You clown." DJ tried to pet her nose, but the frisky filly danced backward and snorted, her ears pricked forward.

"She loves to play, always teases the others until she can get them running after her. Such fun to watch." Jackie leaned on the upper fence rail. "I can't wait until you can come and play with her. Brad wants to put her in a show in early December."

"Not a chance I could handle her by then, but I sure would love to." One of the others came over and let DJ stroke his face. But not Stormy. She'd come just so close, right out of reach, then dance away.

"She moves like a ballerina up on her toes." DJ rested her chin on her hands, which were crossed on the top rail. Maybe if she didn't move, curiosity would overcome her filly. Two others came to inspect DJ, but while Stormy eyed her, she kept her distance. "Silly girl."

"Come on, let's get dinner ready. I'm starved." Jackie

turned away. DJ, with a longing glance over her shoulder, followed.

For Thanksgiving everyone—Gran and Joe; Shawna and her parents, Andy and Sonja; Brad and Jackie—came to their house, bringing all kinds of additions to the turkey that Robert was cooking on the barbecue. They added another table to the one in the dining room so that the thirteen of them, including Maria, could sit together. When all the food covered the table, they took their chairs and joined hands.

"We have an awful lot to be thankful for this year," Joe said from the head of the table. "So you all be thinking, and after we eat, we'll make a family list. But for right now, let's bow our heads." As soon as everyone was quiet, Joe began. "Dear Lord, we come before you with thankful hearts for all you have done for us. We thank you that we live close enough together to be able to enjoy each other's company, to share our sorrows and joys. Thank you that DJ is recovering so wonderfully fast and that soon we'll have a new baby in our circle. For the food before us and our time together we thank you, and most of all for sending us your Son to take away our sins. In Jesus' precious name, amen."

Everyone echoed the *amen*, Billy's the loudest. DJ and Shawna swapped rolled eyes and giggles at the boys' antics. But when DJ looked up at the adults, they all had shiny eyes. Joe's prayer had brought that old familiar lump to her throat, too.

DJ looked across the table when she was passing the mashed potatoes and saw her mother frowning. When DJ raised an eyebrow to ask what was wrong, her mother just shook her head and turned to answer a question from one of the boys. But later when she saw her mother frown again, she began to wonder. *Is she mad about something? This is weird.*

Andy got to teasing the girls, and pretty soon everyone was laughing too hard to pay much attention to anything else. Then Bobby spilled his milk, and Queenie had half of it licked off the floor before Maria could bring the towel.

By the time they finished eating, DJ couldn't tell if she was too full of food or too full of laughter.

"I vote for dessert later." Joe leaned back in his chair and patted his middle. "What I really need right now is a nap."

"I thought we were going to play football." Andy tried to frown, but his eyebrows wouldn't cooperate.

"Yeah, let's play football in the pasture," the boys began to chant.

"We clear the table first." Sonja raised her hands to stop the general exodus. Everyone groaned but began hauling plates and bowls into the kitchen.

"Maria, the dishes wait until after the football game, you hear?" Robert set the turkey platter on the counter. "We'll just put the food away now."

"Sí, Señor. I watch the game, too."

"Where's Mom?" DJ looked around the kitchen and dining room.

"Must have gone to lie down a bit." Robert set the roll of plastic wrap on the counter so they could cover the bowls more easily. "You set them there and I'll rip."

Lindy appeared in the arch of the family room. "No, Robert dear, you won't be ripping. We are on the way to the hospital. My water just broke."

"But the baby's not due for at least two more weeks."

"Maybe not, but it's coming." Lindy turned and headed out to the garage, cupping her belly with both hands.

DJ looked around the room. It looked as if they had all played statue and no one dared move.

Gran returned from the bathroom. "What's the matter?"

"We're having a baby!" Robert looked from his father to Gran. "Oh my goodness, we're going to have a baby. I gotta take her to the hospital. Where're my keys? Someone cover the food." He stared around the kitchen. "Where's Lindy?"

DJ snagged his car keys off the key board by the phone and put them in his hand. "Go! Mom's already in the car." Never had she seen him in such a panic.

Joe started to laugh, grabbed his son by the arm, and hauled him out to the garage.

When he returned, he was still laughing. "My son, the dithering dad. I can't believe that."

"Well, you better believe it, because his wife is my daughter, and we're going to follow them. Anyone, did she have her bag with her?"

DJ thought a moment and shook her head. "I'll get it."

The boys ran in from outside. "When are we playing football?"

DJ left the room in a rush, knowing someone else would answer the boys. The last time she'd seen the bag it had been on the chair by the door of her mother's bedroom. *How come the baby's coming early? Does that mean something is wrong? God, please take care of our baby and Mom.* DJ breathed a sigh of relief to see the overnighter in its right place. She grabbed it and hustled back to the stairs. Joe met her halfway down and took the bag.

"We'll call as soon as we know anything." He planted a quick kiss on the end of her nose and raced out the door after Gran.

"Tell Mom I love her," DJ called after him.

"I will."

DJ continued down the stairs and back to the kitchen, where Jackie had taken over sealing the plates and bowls with plastic wrap. Sonja was finding room in the refrigerator for the leftovers, and what didn't fit there, Maria took to the spare refrigerator in the garage. The boys and Shawna were just bringing in the last things from the table.

"Now, if that isn't the firecracker ending to a Thanksgiving dinner." Andy handed his wife a bowl and snagged a pickle from the plate Brad was clearing off.

"I thought you were stuffed." Sonja gave him her oh-my look.

"I am. I'm eating on nervous energy now. After all, we're having a baby."

"We are?!" Shawna let out a squeal that could be heard clear to the Academy.

"No, dear, not us. He's talking about our extended family here."

"Oh drat."

"You can borrow ours," Bobby said with a totally sober face.

That set Andy off again, and finally even the boys were laughing, though they had no idea at what.

"So when are we gonna play football?" The twins now stood in the doorway, hands on hips.

"We don't have enough players now." DJ looked to Brad, who shrugged.

"No problem." Brad took the boys by their hands. "Come on, let's find the football. It'll help pass the time." As the boys dragged him out to the garage, he called over his shoulder, "You all better get ready."

"I can't play." DJ held up her hands.

"You can cheer for our side." Shawna got behind and pushed her out to the deck. "Come on, Mom, Jackie. We need all the help we can get."

So with Andy on one team and Brad on the other, they chose up sides. Maria played goalpost at one end of the field and DJ at the other. When the score was tied at seven, Brad whispered something to the twin on his team. They went into a huddle with more whispers and giggling.

"All right," Andy hollered. "No fair." Then he bent over

and whispered something to his twin. More giggles.

DJ checked the cell phone she had in her pocket. Sure enough, it was on. But no phone calls. "How long does it take a baby to be born?"

"Long as it takes," Sonja hollered back.

"Big help."

"Okay, ready?" Brad held the ball. They lined up. On the count of three, people ran every direction. Brad threw the ball to his twin, who ran the wrong direction to score a point.

"We won." Andy planted his hands on his hips and puffed.

"No, he ran the wrong way."

"No, he didn't. The twins switched." DJ let out a whoop of laughter, and the twins fell giggling to the ground, the ball between them.

Andy and Brad stared at each other, then at the wives, and they all descended on the boys as Shawna screamed, "Run, Bs, run!"

The boys took off, Queenie yipping and barking after them, the men in hot pursuit.

"Best football game I ever saw." Jackie wiped tears of laughter from her eyes.

"The only one that I wasn't bored to death." Sonja leaned against the fence and flinched as her husband leaped over the dog and landed *splat* in a fresh pile of horse manure. When she dared open her eyes, she looked the other way and asked, "Is he all in one piece, or are we taking another one to the hospital?"

"He's fine."

The cell phone rang, and DJ used both hands to pull it from her pocket. "Hello?" She shook her head at the others, who had frozen in place. "Mom's doing fine, but no baby yet. Thanks, Gran. Tell GJ that Andy fell in the horse poop. That'll make his day."

As they all wandered back to the house, they made Andy walk ten steps behind.

DJ checked the clock. "Shouldn't the baby be born by now?"

"Babies have their own timetable." Sonja pointed her husband toward the bathroom.

"I'll get Andy something to wear." DJ headed for her parents' room. On the way back with jeans and a T-shirt, she glanced in the nursery. Soon they'd have a baby in there.

After eating pumpkin pie and whipped cream, Brad and Jackie gathered up their things to leave. "Now, you call us as soon as you hear anything." Jackie handed DJ their cell phone number.

"I will." DJ hugged them both and, after they said their good-byes to the others, walked them out to their car, the three of them with arms around one another's waists, DJ in the middle. "Thanks for coming."

"I tell you, this is one Thanksgiving we won't forget." Brad turned and kissed DJ's cheek. "And one we have so much to be thankful for. Keep up the good work, DJ. You'll make it."

DJ waved as the Land Rover left the driveway, then hustled back to the kitchen. "Did they call yet?"

When the phone rang a few minutes later, DJ and Sonja reached for it at the same time. This time the call came from one of Robert's men. DJ said she'd give him the message and dictated the number for Andy to write down.

Maria had more coffee dripping when the phone rang again. DJ mentally crossed her fingers.

"We have a baby girl!" Gran announced before DJ could even say hello. DJ relayed the information, and while the others whooped and hollered, she tried to hear Gran's voice. "Mother and daughter are doing fine. Robert about fainted."

DJ hung up, giggling at the picture in her mind of Robert flat on the floor.

DJ took in a deep breath and prayed her "Thank you, God" on a sigh. She didn't realize her shoulders had been nearly pinching her ears until they loosened up after she heard the good news. She called Brad and Jackie to tell them. Then Amy.

"Can you believe it? I have a sister."

"Cool. You're gonna love having a baby sister."

DJ told Amy about the panic of getting Robert in gear and the other funny stories of the afternoon. "My poor mom. There she was sitting in the car waiting for Robert to come drive her. I bet she let him have it."

"When are you coming back to school?"

"I don't know, maybe after Christmas vacation. I'm kinda wishing I could get Mom to homeschool me. That way I could spend more time catching up on my riding— when I finally get to jump again, that is."

"She has a brand-new baby and you want her to homeschool you?" The shock in Amy's voice gave DJ a hint that her idea might not get a very popular reception. "Besides, I really miss you. We had another business club meeting, and I've got a stack of orders again. Did your mom find out about that group to package our cards?"

"Got me. If she did, the information will be in her file. I'll look tomorrow."

"Good, 'cause we gotta get on this."

DJ groaned.

"Hey, what did they name the baby?"

"Ahh." DJ tried to remember which of the many discussed names they had finally agreed on, or *if* they had agreed. "They couldn't make up their minds. A boy would have been Jeffrey Allan, so the girl is either Amanda Marie or . . . or . . ." *Come on, brain, get in motion.* "I don't remember."

"Some sister you are."

Later, DJ hung up with those words in her mind. *Yeah, some sister I am.* She went in to play Go Fish with the twins. *At least I can do that right.*

Gran and Joe came back a bit later when DJ was just getting the boys ready for bed. Maria was fixing snacks. Supervising the boys was supposed to be easier. At least it didn't matter that her hands couldn't pick up small things. They fit around each boy's hands as she dragged them into the bathroom to brush their teeth. They still had the giggles, an everyday occurrence with them.

"DJ?" Gran called.

"Up here. Okay, hustle it, you two. I want another piece of pumpkin pie. And Gran and Joe are here if you want to say good-night."

"Why can't they stay here?"

"Why should they? Maria and I are here."

Bobby turned to Billy, Billy turned to Bobby, and off they went again, toothpaste trailing from their brushes to the sink.

"Enough!" DJ made the time-out sign. "Knock it off or no bedtime story." She glared at them, trying her hardest to keep frowning even though she would rather giggle along with them. But with any encouragement, they *would* giggle all night.

They brushed, and spit, and rinsed, and raced into their pj's, then bolted down the stairs to throw themselves at Gran and Joe. By the time DJ made it down the stairs herself, Joe had a twin under each arm, threatening to dump them in the birdbath.

"How's Mom?"

"Tired but wonderfully happy. You have the most beautiful baby sister."

"Prettier than Stormy?"

"Oh, you." Gran swatted her on the rear and finished off

with a hug. "What a circus that was here. I've heard of dithering dads, but I didn't expect it of Robert."

"You have to admit, this caught us all by surprise."

"I know. Here we were thinking that if it came a bit late,
we would have a Christmas baby. And instead she came at
Thanksgiving."

"Maybe we should name her Turkey." DJ sidestepped another swat.

"Not funny. Robert is already calling her his little pumpkin."

"Gran." DJ lowered her voice. "What did they finally
name her? Even yesterday Mom still wasn't sure."

"Amanda Marie. Isn't that pretty? Just like her."

"Good, that's the one I liked best." DJ took her pumpkin
pie foaming with whipped cream and sat on a stool at the
counter. "Thanks, Maria." She could hear Joe and the boys
laughing in the family room as she cut off a bite and ate it.
If what Amy said about new babies was true, life was going
to be different around here. But how? And how much?

"I love babies," Maria said.

"Me too. The more grandkids, the better." Gran wore a
sappy look that made DJ shake her head. What was so wonderful about babies? At least foals get on their feet within
the first hour.

15

"ALL SHE DOES IS SLEEP."

"Sometimes she cries."

"But not much. Amanda is really a happy baby." Lindy held the sleeping infant down for the boys to bestow their nightly kisses on the rounded forehead of their two-week-old baby sister.

"You said we got a baby sister to play with." Bobby's tone held accusation. Billy nodded in total agreement.

"One of these days . . ." Lindy kissed each of her sons. "Go get your baths, and I'll be in to kiss you good-night."

"When's Daddy coming home?" Bobby always came up with one more question to put off going to bed. Robert had left for a business trip three days earlier.

DJ recognized the ploy; she'd used it often enough herself. "Day after tomorrow. Come on, guys, hit the tub." The twins, after one more beseeching look that earned them a headshake from their mother, tore down the hall and, running into the bathroom, slapped the tub.

"We hit it." Unison again.

DJ paused in the doorway and rolled her eyes. "You two are too much." She turned on the water to the right temperature and waited until they were in before going to their bedroom for the book she'd promised to read—if they washed behind their ears. *The Cat in the Hat.* Are you sure this is the one you want? You have it about memorized."

"Read." Pause. They looked at each another in silent communication, then in unison said, "Please." More matching giggles.

By the time DJ finished the story, the boys' fingers had wrinkled and they were ready to get out. DJ enjoyed reading the book to them as much as they loved to be read to. She could remember Gran reading it to her.

"Okay, put your toys in the sling and your towels on the rods—no, fold them first, you know how. There, good. Oh, come on, clothes in the hamper."

"I want to wear my jeans tomorrow."

"Gross, they're filthy. You've got more jeans."

"But I like those best." Bobby stuck out his bottom lip.

"Tough." She put a hand behind each head and guided them out of the bathroom and into their bedroom. When they were in bed, she bent and gave each a kiss. "Nighty-night. I'll get Mom."

"Sleep tight, DJ."

She headed down the hall to her parents' wing. Lindy was just tucking Amanda back in the crib. She patted the baby's back and turned out the light. "They're ready?"

"As they'll ever be. I already read their story."

"Thanks for telling me. Last night they worked in two." Lindy laid her arm across DJ's shoulders. "Have I ever told you how much I love you?"

DJ grinned. "Once or twice." She put her arm around her mother's waist. "Guess you never hear it too much, right?"

"I'll be in after I hear their prayers and read our verses."

DJ peeled off at her bedroom door and stared with longing at the pad of drawing paper she'd dug out of the drawer. "One of these days." She squeezed her hands together, then set the fingertips of both hands together and pushed, bent, and pushed. No matter how much she bent and stretched them, it never seemed to be enough.

With her utmost concentration, DJ could touch her fingers to her thumbs, but any automatic coordination between them all still was not there. At least she could turn pages easily now, and most of the time her mind kept track of things, so studying had become almost normal.

That is, unless she had to write notes or the answers on a test. Or any test, for that matter. The pressure seemed to bring on confusion. And art was still out of the question. Now that she rode every day, drawing and jumping were the two things she really missed—so badly that sometimes it felt like her heart hurt with wanting.

She left off the exercises when her mom walked into her room and sat down on the end of the bed. "Thanks for helping with the boys."

"You're welcome." DJ took the drawing pad from her bed and put it back in the drawer.

"You've tried drawing?"

DJ shrugged. "Some, but nothing's coming yet. Even with the foam on them, I can't seem to work a pencil right. I'm going to have to buy my Christmas presents. I had planned to make most of them."

Lindy cocked her head. "Do I hear Amanda crying?"

"Uh-huh." DJ leaned over and kissed her mother's cheek. "Bet she's hungry again."

"She's a little pig, that's what. She'd nurse twenty-four hours a day, I think." Lindy pushed herself to her feet. "No wonder God gives babies to younger mothers. They have more stamina." She leaned against the doorjamb. "Don't worry about presents, DJ. People will understand, you know."

"I know. It's just that I like to see people open presents I made."

142

"So," Bridget said the next afternoon, "are you ready to jump?"

"Am I ready? Did the sun get up this morning? Does a horse sweat?"

"I get the picture. See you in the jumping ring in ten—no, better make it fifteen minutes."

If DJ's feet touched the ground between the office and Megs' stall, she never knew it. She groomed Megs in record time, saddled and bridled her, then snagged someone to tighten the girth and the throat latch on the bridle. Finally she'd regained her ability to use the hoof-pick. While she could now hold the reins properly—most of the time—she still lacked the strength and coordination to be able to squeeze and release the reins. The fear of a runout still stuck holes in her confidence at times.

She'd tried mounting without the block the day before, but her hands didn't have the strength to hold on to the saddle while she pulled herself up. But they were getting there. *Soon*, she'd promised herself. *Soon*.

DJ rode Megs out to the ring and worked on the flat at a walk, trot, and canter while she waited for Bridget. The jumps were still low from her previous class as the teacher. Her two ladies were coming along just fine and having a great time. They called DJ names like "ogre" and "general," so she knew she was being strict enough with them.

DJ worked around the ring, reverse and walk, trot, canter again, circles, turns, and halts, then on to the cavalletti bars with a walk and trot again, all to perfect her timing.

"Sorry I am late. The phone got me." Bridget let herself in the aluminum-rail gate and crossed to the center of the ring. "All right, nice and easy, trot the cavalletti. Do not rush. There is no hurry."

DJ swallowed her butterflies, trotted Megs over the cavalletti, and popped over the low jump Bridget had set up at the end of the bars. They picked up a canter, DJ counted *three, two, one*, and while Megs scarcely noticed the effort, DJ felt that brief moment of flying. Her eyes blurred. She wanted to scream and shout, but instead blinked her eyes clear and counted the paces until the next jump. They completed the round of five jumps as tears streamed down her face. "I'm jumping again! Thank you, God. I am jumping again." It was all she could do to stay in the saddle. Doing a Snoopy dance all around the barns sounded like a fun thing, about the only thing that could show how she felt.

Was that the sheen of tears DJ saw in Bridget's eyes, too? DJ stopped Megs so she could dry her eyes on the sleeve of her sweat shirt. She leaned forward and hugged the aging mare. "Thank you, old girl, for putting up with me. I know I wasn't perfect, but you have no idea . . ."

"You did well for all you have been through. Were you dizzy at all?"

"Not then, but I think I am now. Dizzy with pure joy. Do you get dizzy from that?"

"A different kind, but I think so. Your face is glowing, DJ. I am so happy for you that I cannot begin to tell of it. This has surely stretched my faith, too, and I thank our God for saving you and bringing you back to ride again."

DJ could only nod, her throat too tight to speak.

"Now, are you ready to go again?" Bridget waited for DJ's nod. "You were a little behind on one and ahead on another, so now maybe you can focus on the jumping along with the joy."

DJ nodded again before signaling Megs to take another round. This time she was able to pay more attention to her body and the fine-tuning that she needed. She counted the paces, made sure her mind didn't wander, and always looked ahead to the next jump. Megs hesitated the tiniest bit at the in and out but cleared it with no problem. With low jumps like they were doing, it wasn't so bad, but DJ knew her hesitance was enough to cause a bar to go down on a competition jump.

When they finished the final round, clapping broke out from outside the ring. Bunny Ellsindorf, Tony Andrada, and a couple of others laughed and cheered. "Yay, DJ, you did it! You're jumping again. Way to go."

DJ waved and stopped next to Bridget.

Bridget patted her knee. "How do your hands feel?"

"Tender, but not sore." DJ dismounted since she could just swing her leg over and slide to the ground. She flexed her hands. "I keep working with the squeeze-me's and I can tell a difference each week, but I have a ways to go yet."

"Squeeze-me's?"

"Those little rubbery bead-filled thingies. I've worn the rubber right off two of them. Of course, Queenie catching one the boys threw didn't help it much. They're better than the ball the therapist started me with."

"Whatever it takes. That is one good thing about you, DJ—you do whatever it takes."

"Thank you." DJ marveled all the way back to the barn and on home at the compliment Bridget had given her. Compliments from Bridget were far better than trophies any day.

"I think you can go back to school with the new semester," Debra, the tutor, said on the last study day before Christmas vacation. "We'll set your schedule for as much as you can handle at first, and with foam around pens and pencils, plus some other adaptations, you should be fine. Just spend time practicing your writing over vacation, and I'll see you after the first of the year."

DJ didn't mention she was hoping to talk her mother

into homeschooling her, but in case she refused, the thought of going back to school pulled her forehead into a frown.

"You don't agree?"

DJ shrugged. What was there to say?

"What bothers you? You concentrate well again—except for when you get too tired—your hands are improving all the time, your hair is cute as can be . . ."

"I don't know. It's just scary, I guess."

"Well, don't worry about it, and have a merry Christmas." Debra dug in her bag and brought out a package wrapped in red and gold paper. "Not much, but I thought of you when I saw it."

"Thank you. Do I need to wait till Christmas to open it?"

"Of course." Her dark eyes twinkled. "And thank you for being such a good student."

"You're welcome." DJ crossed to a stack of presents that looked as if the boys had wrapped them—only without as much tape. "This is for you. Sorry the wrapping isn't better."

"Can I open it?"

"If I can open mine."

"Okay, on three. One, two, three."

DJ used her teeth for the first rip, then got the box unwrapped. Pulling off the lid, she found tissue paper and finally a Christmas tree ornament of a jumping horse.

"This is a picture you did?" Debra asked.

DJ looked up to nod. "That's Stormy, my filly, when she was only a couple of weeks old."

The framed pencil drawing showed the filly peeking out from behind her dam, her mother's tail feathering across her little face and pointed ears.

"She's beautiful. Look at the mischief dancing in her eyes. DJ, you are an incredible artist. Thank you so very much." Debra clasped the picture to her chest. "I'll always treasure this."

At least I was *an artist*. DJ smiled in spite of the thought. "And me this. How perfect."

DJ walked Debra downstairs, where Maria met them with a plastic-wrapped plate of Christmas goodies.

"Here, this for you. *Feliz Navidad*."

"Gracias, Maria, and feliz Navidad to you, too. Did you make all these?"

"Sí."

"What a treat. Merry Christmas and happy New Year, DJ, and tell all your family for me, too."

After she left, DJ ambled into the kitchen. "Gracias, Maria. And thanks, too. That was really nice of you."

"She help you much. Need cookies."

"How about me?"

Maria rolled her eyes and opened a plastic container for DJ, who helped herself to two Mexican wedding cakes, one of her favorite cookies.

"See, I can even hold them." DJ popped one of the powdered-sugar-coated cookies into her mouth. "But I don't hold them for long."

Amanda Marie Crowder took top billing in the Christmas pageant at church, playing the role of baby Jesus. And like an angel, she slept right through the whole thing.

The twins, however, were a different matter. One lost his halo, the other his harp. They and the other angels sang "Hello, Baby Jesus" around the manger.

"That's my baby sister."

Those sitting clear at the back of the sanctuary heard the whispered comment clearly.

It took a while for the congregation to stop laughing so the next lines could be heard.

Two days later DJ had a rampaging case of butterflies.

The Christmas Eve candlelight service would be the test. Last year she'd gone catatonic when they lit their candles. She'd scared the twins half to bits.

"Not to worry, darlin'," Gran said when DJ whispered her fears at dinner. "You will never be afraid of fire again. You've been healed, remember?"

DJ looked at her hands. "The hard way, for sure."

"But healed nonetheless."

DJ remembered Gran's words as she dipped her candle over Robert's and the flame grew. How beautiful that small, flickering light that she held for Joe to light from. She looked from her candle to Joe and then to Robert. Both wore grins wide enough to catch the tears that glistened in their eyes. GJ hugged her from one side and Robert from the other. Gran reached around Joe and patted her knee.

"You were right," DJ stage-whispered while everyone sang "Silent Night."

"I know. Thank you, Jesus."

"Amen to that." The two men spoke as one.

Of all her presents, that one was the greatest.

DJ and Amy spent three days of their vacation up at Brad and Jackie's, playing with the yearlings. Stormy and DJ made friends again the first day, and Amy took lots of pictures of the little ham.

"She sees that camera and puts on an attitude." Amy shook her head. "She will love the show-ring."

"Her confirmation is near perfect, too. She's one of the best fillies Matadorian has sired." Brad rested his elbows on the top of a fence post. "Seems his colts do better than the fillies."

"Why is that?" DJ asked. The three of them were leaning on the white board fence watching the horse kids play. She turned to watch her father's face.

"Not sure, but she broke the male pattern. Even her color is different. But she has his fire all right."

During their stay, DJ worked up to riding Herndon without the lunge line. She hadn't jumped yet, just worked him on the flat in the indoor arena. Somehow she felt safer in there, as if there might not be as much to distract him. Since he nickered whenever he saw her coming, DJ always kept horse cookies in her sweat shirt pouch. The day he helped himself, with a little help from her, Amy snorted.

"I can't believe it. Someone must have exchanged another horse for Herndon."

"Cross my heart, same horse." Jackie made the motions.

"Do . . . do you think he's lost his edge? His style has always set him so apart in the ring." DJ had been wondering but was hesitant to ask.

"I don't think so. He still loves an audience, and the two of you go marvelously together. Want me to set up a couple of low jumps to pop over?"

DJ swallowed. "I . . . I guess." Her butterflies whooped and hollered, as only internal butterflies can.

But jumping Herndon was like jumping Megs, only far better. He took the jumps without even a snort, his ears flicking back and forth, listening for DJ's commands. She kept her hands firm on the foam-covered reins, and while she drove him forward into her hand, he was featherlight, almost sensing the tenderness of DJ's hands.

"You know what?" Jackie stood at Herndon's shoulder, looking up at DJ. "This may sound strange, but in a way, your hand injury is a good thing. The stronger your legs and the lighter your hands, the more Herndon responds for the good."

DJ made a face and flexed her right hand. "You think so?"

"Nope, I don't just *think* so. I know so."

"So when do you want Herndon back at Briones?" Brad asked on their way back to Pleasant Hill.

"Next weekend?" DJ gulped when she said it. Now he would be all her responsibility again. Would she be able to handle it all?

"Done. You want me to bring Stormy, too?"

"What?"

"Don't worry, I'm teasing. But I do want you to train her if you can fit it in. You have a good sense of the best way to train different horses, and since she is yours, I thought you might want to do that."

"I never thought about that."

"We have plenty of time. She has a lot of growing to do, but when the time comes, we'll talk again. I'll pay for her board and all the vet bills and such."

"Th-thank you."

"You lucky dog," Amy said when Brad drove away. "You have two horses."

"How will I ever do all that? Train me, train a new horse . . ." She glanced down at her hands. "Train my hands to hold a pencil again?"

"You will. Have you tried drawing yet?"

"Huh-uh." DJ led the way up to her room, pausing in the doorway. "What if I can't?" Her voice broke on the forbidden word. The fear had dug itself in deep.

"You'll never know until you try. I'm surprised you haven't already."

"Now you sound like Gran."

"Good."

That night DJ locked the fear in a box and took out a pad of drawing paper and several pencils. But even the one wrapped in foam went every which way until she threw it across the room. The fear leaped from its box and threw her across her bed to drown in her tears.

The Sunday after New Years, DJ and her mother were bathing Amanda, who took to the water like a baby dolphin. She smiled and cooed every time, waving her arms and kicking her legs as if she were ready to take off.

"Here, you dry her. The towel is over there." Lindy nodded toward the rod. When DJ held out her hands, buried in the towel, Lindy scooped up the dripping baby and deposited her in the pink towel. She tucked the ends around her baby daughter and kissed the cheek of her older one. "Isn't she the most precious thing you ever saw?"

"Yep, almost as good as Stormy." DJ giggled her way back to the changing table in the baby's room. Seeing the look on her mother's face was always such fun.

"I suppose you want powder, too?" DJ dried the tiny fingers and toes. Manda, as she'd quickly become, reached for DJ's face and smiled, her blue eyes wide. "Don't tell Mom, but you *are* even better than Stormy."

"I heard that."

DJ powdered the baby and reached for a disposable diaper. "Mom, I can't do the diaper thing." Pulling the tabs off the sticky paper was beyond her fingers' ability yet.

"Be right there." Lindy finished the job and handed the baby back to DJ. "I'll be done with the printer in a minute if you can take her that long."

"No prob." DJ, baby in arms, followed her mother into the office, where Lindy was printing out copies of her manuscript for a couple of her friends to read and look for problems. When the last section finished printing, Lindy took the stack of papers and tapped the bottom edge on the desk to straighten them. She set them down with a sigh. "Wow, what a job."

"It reads good, though."

"Well."

DJ rolled her eyes. "Well, reads *well*." She sat in the chair by the window and played with the baby's fingers. *Ask her now. No, wait.* The voices were too much. "Mom, I've been thinking . . ."

Lindy stopped moving things around on her desk. "And?"

"And I was wondering if maybe you would homeschool me next semester?" There, it was out. She didn't even dare look at her mother.

16

THE FIRST WEEK OF THE NEW QUARTER DJ attended Acalanese High School only half days.

"It feels strange," she answered in response to her mother's question the third afternoon. "And I'm beat, but I know it will get better."

"I'm sorry, DJ, about not feeling I can homeschool you. I've prayed and Robert's prayed and Gran, too. We all feel this is the best."

"I know. Guess it was a long shot, but that way I thought I could do it all."

"Do what all?" Lindy swayed from side to side with Manda in her arms.

"Oh, train and teach and school and the cards and—"

"Well, as we agreed, teaching is out until you feel up to it again. We can cut more if need be. Are you still angry?"

"Nope, not now. I know it's for the best." DJ munched on the baby carrots and other veggies Maria had set out, along with the chocolate chip cookies. It had taken her a few days to reach that point of acceptance, but it helped when Bridget totally agreed with her parents. The girls from her riding class groaned loud enough to scare the horses, but they were so glad to have her back in the barns that they switched to laughter pretty quickly.

School really had gone better than DJ thought it would. Other kids treated her like a celebrity for a day or so, and no one stared at her hands or her short hair. Even that had grown enough so that DJ could get a new style at the salon. The only bad thing: She still couldn't take art class. She'd had to take study hall instead. Art had been the highlight of her days before.

Everything was *before* or *after.*

"I gotta get changed and over to the barns, Mom. Joe asked if I would take care of Ranger, too."

"He went to San Francisco with Gran, then?"

"Um." DJ snagged another cookie and drained her milk. "Tell the boys to get General's stall cleaned out, and I'll try to be home before dark so they can ride." She dropped a kiss on Manda's cheek and another on the waving pink fist. "What a sweetie you are, Manda Banda."

"DJ, her name is Amanda Marie." But the laughter in Lindy's voice took away any reproof. "Remember that tomorrow you have an appointment with the therapist."

"I know." DJ threw the words over her shoulder as she took the stairs three at a time. Halfway up she stopped and yelled back, "Some girl stopped me today to tell me what a cool haircut I had. Said she might do one like it."

"You might start a new fad."

"Me? Ha, what a joke."

Bridget had DJ back to riding two classes on the flat and one of low jumping every week.

"Just until you get stronger, although Jackie kept Herndon in excellent condition. The jumping will come again. You must be patient."

DJ groaned inside but kept a smile on her face. "I know." Even as she stood in Bridget's office, she kept working her fingers, pushing them into her palm with the opposite hand. She seemed to have reached a plateau with no noticeable improvement in dexterity. [...] normal, but . . .

January seemed to be a m[...] At least, that's the way it seer[...] the riders in the covered aren[...] herself to gain more strength[...] she rode on the off days.

"You need to take it easier, [...]

"I will." But the next day DJ could [...] her leg grip. Herndon swerved to the inside, and since [...] was tight and not sitting deep in the saddle, DJ found herself on the ground. "Oof." She thought more words than that. Her hands stung, her rear stung, and she wanted to scream.

"Put him away."

DJ closed her eyes. Why did Bridget have to catch her like this?

"No riding tomorrow. I warned you." While the voice was gentle, steel underscored it.

Without answering, DJ put Herndon away. "Sorry, big horse. This wasn't your fault." *It was my fault. And I should know better.* She called herself several names on the way out to the truck.

Bridget met her at the barn door. "You will not beat up on yourself either, will you, ma petite?"

"No." But she had the grace to look caught. "I'm sorry."

"I know you are, but we will get through this, too. You have come a long way. Do not be in such a rush. That is when accidents happen."

"What was that about?" Joe asked when he climbed in the pickup.

DJ told him what happened.

"Did you hurt your hands?"

DJ shrugged. "Not really. But my pride sure stings."

"The inside one or the one you sit on?"

e couldn't help but laugh.

er when they finally got to return to the out-
dropped the reins just as she and Herndon ap-
a jump. He stopped and she didn't.

ew you'd do that one of these times," she muttered
led him back to the mounting block. No matter how
Herndon behaved now, she kept expecting him to act
p like he used to. She tried flexing her hands, and the
strength wasn't there. Too tired. DJ gritted her teeth and
mounted again.

"Slow canter around the ring outside the jumps, then
trot the cavalletti. Next week we will do a grid. You just
have to be more patient with yourself." Bridget gave her a
shrugging smile.

DJ spent the month of February working on a lot of flatwork; the grid, which was made up of seven even jumps
with two paces between and was designed to rebuild confidence; strides and balance; and attempted drawings that
made it no farther than the wastebasket. The rain continued.

"I feel like someone sure is raining on my parade," DJ
told her grandmother one night on the phone.

Gran chuckled. "Don't we all. Here I'm trying to paint
sunny meadows, and we keep getting black clouds."

"And don't tell me this, too, shall pass."

"I won't. You just said it."

"G-r-a-n." But DJ couldn't help but smile. She'd stepped
right into that trap. "Got a verse for me?"

"Ah, how about Noah on the ark, when it rained for
forty days and nights?"

"Thanks a big fat bunch."

"But the skies finally cleared and the dove brought back
a green branch. Good night, darlin'."

The next afternoon a hand-painted card awaited DJ on the kitchen counter. Inside was an ark with a man in a long beard, reaching for the branch from a white dove. The sun shone and a rainbow arched over the ark. Inside it read *Even Noah thought it might rain forever. But it didn't. I love you. Gran.*

DJ handed it to her mother. "Cool, huh?"

"She just whipped this up, right?" Lindy sighed. "Such talent between you and her. Sometimes I'm jealous. I think we should frame this."

DJ agreed. And tried to think of rainbows instead of the rain.

"So how is your attitude?" Bridget asked as she opened the gate to let DJ out of the arena.

Needs a bath. "I'm working on it."

"I think we will leave the grids next week and return to regular jumps."

DJ could feel her attitude shifting almost miraculously. Surely March would be better than the weeks before. "The grid helped, though, didn't it?" She didn't need Bridget to answer. She felt not only stronger, but more sure of Herndon and of herself.

That night DJ tore down the stairs, holding out a drawing tablet. "Mom, look!"

"What?! Oh my word, you scared me half to death." She held her hand to her heart.

"What is it, darlin'?"

"Hey, Gran, I didn't know you were here." DJ crossed to the small glass table and antiqued iron chairs set up by the French doors so her mother could see the backyard in spite of the March rains. "This." She moved the pot of ruby tulips out of the way and laid her drawing pad on the table between the two women.

The half-grown horse was obviously Stormy. She seemed to be reaching so far for something that she was standing on her tiptoes but at the same time gave the impression she would flee at any moment.

Gran picked it up and tilted it toward the light. "Wonderful. Such feeling and motion. When did you do this?"

"I just finished it. I've been working with the pencils for weeks, and the first ones were terrible. But I got what I wanted here. That's the way she was when Amy and I were up there during Christmas break." She didn't tell them about the wastebaskets full of failures.

Gran handed the drawing to Lindy and reached an arm around DJ's waist. "Well, I do think you can get over worrying about your artwork. You didn't lose your touch."

"Or else I found it again. I was worried there for a while."

"DJ, darlin', I think you've found a lot more than your drawing touch."

"Like what?"

"Oh, you're more sensitive than ever, not only in your fingers but perhaps in your heart, mind, and soul. You think?"

DJ shrugged. She hadn't thought about that, but like Bridget, Gran was almost always right.

"Oh, DJ, I can't believe this." Lindy shook her head slowly, smiling all the while. "I have a suggestion. How about we make prints of this, frame them, and give one to Dr. Niguri, one to Nurse Karen, and one to your therapist, Jody. They would really appreciate seeing the outcome of their handiwork."

"I was thinking of blowing it up for Robert and Brad for Father's Day." It felt funny saying Dad and Dad, so she'd used their names, but that felt funny, too.

"How about for your grandfather, too? He'd love one."

"Maybe I ought to go into production. So do you think I'm ready to go back into art class when the new quarter begins in a couple of weeks?"

"I think so. Simply amazing."

"Thank you, heavenly Father, for all your mercies on our dear girl." Gran studied the drawing again.

"Amen to that. I've been thanking Him. Of course, it is easier now that things are better, but I tried to in the bad times, too."

"I know you did. Let's do these on real good paper. How about asking your grandfather if he would like to do the frames for the two big ones? He'd be so proud you asked."

"Good, then I'll take his down to the frame shop." DJ gave her mother and grandmother each a hug.

"Oh, DJ, before you run off. The woman from Outlook House called, and they have the cards packaged and ready to be picked up. All ten boxes. And they shrink-wrapped the singles and the prints. Not sure how many more boxes that makes."

"Ten boxes. Did we really order that many?" DJ sank onto the other chair.

"You're going to need warehouse space pretty soon at the rate you're going." Gran sat back and sipped her licorice tea.

"And someone to do the shipping."

"I can't believe this." DJ looked down at the drawing. This one could possibly be included in the next printing. She traced her finger around the edge of the tablet. Who would have dreamed that their little card idea would grow like this? Being able to draw again, no matter how slowly, made up in part for the weeks of rain and sloggy flatwork.

"One month until the first show." Tony Andrada stared at the March calendar on the wall. "Do you think you'll be ready?" He turned to DJ, one eyebrow raised like a question mark.

"I have to be." But Bridget still had her schooling over low jumps, nothing like competition. "Bridget suggested I enter Hunter classes this first time."

"That's good. You can call the first time in the ring again a schooling show."

"I guess."

"Trust her, she knows the best way."

"She sure does," Hilary Jones joined in. "She has me scheduled for a show in Las Vegas next weekend and Phoenix two weeks after that. My dad is going to trailer my horse, and I'll fly there so I don't miss so much school. You think high school is hard, wait until you hit college."

DJ knew Brad was hoping she could help him show in Phoenix the end of April, but that was different from jumping Herndon. Her mother had reserved the final decision for DJ, depending on her energy level and how school was going. If not, well, there'd be another time.

The first show rolled into reality faster than DJ dreamed it would. Herndon walked out of the trailer as if he owned the world and whinnied to let his subjects know he'd arrived.

"Right in my ear." DJ smacked his shoulder, more like a love pat. If only he could scare away the butterflies in her middle with his piercing whinny. They'd even taken to waking her up at night.

Herndon turned to look at her, snuffled her hair, and resumed his aristocratic pose. But he walked beside her to his stall without pulling at the rope or dancing any of his mighty jigs. When they were warming up in the schooling arena, he watched the others but didn't feel like a wire stretched to the point of snapping. He popped over the schooling jumps without pulling or rushing his fences, and his ears pricked—evidence that he was having a good time.

So was DJ, except for the inner butterfly battle.

DJ wore riding gloves now, her Jobst gloves in her bag for later. She'd been able to do without them for several hours a day lately, but it felt strange without them. They were somewhat tighter than leather riding gloves. She flexed her hands, one at a time, keeping the reins secure in the other. *Please, God, let him behave. I don't care if we get a single ribbon. I just want to do well and get over these awful butterflies.* She'd awakened that morning feeling like she had to throw up. Not a good start for the day.

Herndon danced sideways, reacting to DJ's nervousness, until DJ tightened both legs and hands and trotted forward.

They placed fifth in Junior Working Hunter Under Saddle, but DJ didn't feel bad. She'd entered it on Bridget's orders, and now they were over their first hurdle—entering a show-ring again.

"To give you more experience," Bridget had said firmly.

Junior Hunter Seat Equitation Under Saddle earned them a red. Herndon had turned on the charm and caught everyone's attention, including the judge.

Junior Hunter Over Fences had three of them in close competition. When DJ was awarded the yellow—third place—Joe grumbled, "Politics, that's what. That judge must have been having eye trouble."

"Joe Crowder." Gran slapped his arm with her program. "Don't you talk like that."

DJ chuckled at the guilty look on her grandfather's face. "Gotcha, didn't she?"

DJ rode third in her next class. When her number was called, she leaned forward in the saddle, took a deep breath, let it all out, and signaled Herndon into a trot. Entering the ring, she circled, asked him for a canter, and then they headed for the first jump, a single post and rail. He cleared it like he did all the others, with room to spare. They went around twice, then out.

"He was just playing out there." DJ stroked his neck. "Didn't even break a sweat." But the feeling had been there, the feeling of flying. *I can fly again. I know we could do the Jumper class.*

The crowd cheered, especially her own cheering section of family and the gang from Briones, as DJ trotted back out to accept the blue ribbon for first. Herndon acted as if it were all for him, and he graciously accepted the accolades.

"He's a big ham, that's what."

"You did good, DJ. You were the best." The boys leaned around their father, who had their hands tightly secured in his own.

"Thanks, guys." Since DJ was done showing, she put Herndon in his stall and came back to the arena to watch the jumping classes. When Tony Andrada entered the ring, he winked at her and then took first with only one jump-off.

"You gotta get back out there so I have someone to compete against. That was way too easy," Tony said when they were packing up to leave. He leaned his elbow on his knee, with one foot up on the closed burgundy-painted chest that held their tack. Two girls walked past, giggling as they went.

"Your fan club, Tony. Aren't you impressed?"

"Yeah, right. All I need right now." He took a swig from his can of soda and stretched his neck from side to side. "So the next one is May first at Rancho de Equus. You're going, right?"

DJ felt her stomach hit her boot tops. Rancho de Equus—the scene of the fire.

17

"YOU DON'T HAVE TO DO IT, darlin'," Gran told DJ on the last Thursday in April—two days before the show at Rancho de Equus.

"I know, Gran, but I think I need to. Just pray for me, please. I think my butterflies invited in a whole new flock. There's a battle going on inside me."

"No doubt. But there will be other shows. You can wait."

DJ nodded. "But I am going." She forced herself to sound more certain. "I *am* going. We leave tomorrow afternoon, as soon as everyone gets to the Academy. Joe said he would take me earlier to beat the traffic, but that's not fair to the others. At least we're not on the early program on Saturday morning." DJ knew she was chattering, but if she kept talking her teeth didn't clatter together.

She might just as well have stayed home from school Friday for all her concentration on the lessons. Except in art class. She wouldn't miss that for anything. But the metallic taste in her mouth made lunch taste so bad she quit eating.

The drive south wasn't as bad as they'd thought it might

be. They hit San Jose at the end of the traffic and sailed right on to the horse park. *Rancho de Equus* in black metal letters arched over the entrance, bordered by tall stucco walls on each side. Bright red roses bloomed along the lower sections of the walls and around the fences.

DJ took in a deep breath as they drove under the sign. This would be a good show this time. It had to be. The jitters in her fingers traveled up her arms.

They checked all their horses in without any difficulty, this time assigned to an entirely different barn than she'd been in last fall. DJ looked over to where barn D had been. A brand-new white barn stood in the place of the one that had burned down.

"Did you see that?" She nodded in the new barn's direction when talking with Hilary.

"Sure looks better than the old one. Did they ever find out what started the fire?"

"Got me." DJ shook her head and shuddered. "I'm glad it's all rebuilt. Makes this easier somehow."

But sleep that night in the motor home wasn't easy. She woke twice with the nightmare. Once she must have screamed or something because Bunny came to check on her.

"You all right, DJ?" She kept her voice low so she wouldn't wake up the others.

"I will be. Haven't had these dreams for a long time." DJ swung her feet to the floor. "Guess I'll get a drink and go to the bathroom. Thanks for coming, but I'm sorry to have bothered you."

Bunny pushed her hair behind her ear. "No matter, just so you're all right. And no sneaking out, you hear?"

"I won't. If I hear anything, I'll yell loud enough to wake all of you."

Bunny chuckled her way back to her own bed.

DJ was cleaning out Herndon's stall the next morning

when one of the officials approached her. "Are you DJ Randall?"

"Yes." *What did I do wrong now?*

"We wanted to make sure you and your horse are going to be part of the opening ceremonies. We'd like you to ride right behind the colors."

"Well, sure, but why—?"

"Good, we'll see you then."

"What was that all about?" Tony stopped his wheelbarrow next to her.

"Got me. But that means I better hustle. I wasn't planning on being dressed by then."

True to her word, DJ, Herndon, and her butterflies were ready to go when the announcer welcomed the crowd. She'd already seen her parents, including baby Amanda since Lindy was still nursing her, and the twins, Gran, Brad and Jackie, and Shawna and her family. The Crowders were out in full force. DJ waved back at the twins and took her place behind the color guard.

"Glad to see you back here," the ring superintendent said and reached up to shake her hand.

"Thank you." DJ remembered her manners, but what was the big deal?

"Hey, DJ."

She turned to look and saw a familiar nurse with a certain fireman's arm around her shoulders. "Karen, Allen, hi. How'd you know about this?"

"We'll tell you later." They waved.

The music started and the parade began. Three men in full Mexican regalia held the standards for the American flag, the California flag with the bear on it, and the Rancho flag. They trotted into the arena and DJ followed. Behind her came a riding team, and behind that many of the other entrants.

The color guard circled and stopped to face the audience, who all stood at the beginning of the "Star Spangled Banner." DJ watched the flag snapping in the breeze and listened to the song sung by a young boy with a mighty powerful voice. When he finished, she waited for the color guard to canter out, but they stayed in place. So she did, too. DJ looked to her left, and the rider there shrugged back.

Herndon shifted from one foot to the other. "Easy, fella, this will be over soon."

"Welcome, folks, to the spring show at Rancho de Equus, the premier horse park of California. We have something special today, so make yourselves comfortable for a few minutes. Last August we had a near tragedy here that was averted by the quick thinking and incredible courage of a young woman. One of our barns caught on fire. When DJ Randall smelled the smoke, she threw the fire alarm and, without thought for her own safety, managed to save all the horses in that barn. She came terribly close to losing her life, but she is here with us today and riding Herndon, who was also in the fire."

I think I'm going to faint or cry or . . .

"Would you please ride forward, Miss Randall?"

DJ did as asked. The applause and cheering thundered around the arena.

"Many of you might have noticed the new barn raised in place of the burned one. While we call it barn D, we have here a brass plaque that will be attached to the wall by the front door as you enter the barn. It says, 'The DJ Randall Barn. Dedicated to DJ Randall for saving six horses from burning with no thought to her own safety. We thank her and name this barn in her honor.' "

"We have a matching plaque for you, DJ, with our deepest thanks."

A woman walked toward DJ and handed her a thin box wrapped in gold paper. She shook DJ's hand and said, "One of those horses you saved was mine. I can never thank you enough."

"Y-you're welcome."

"You'll find in that package a slight token of our esteem, DJ, and God bless you," the announcer finished to a standing ovation.

DJ let the tears flow. She had no choice.

When the crowd sat down again, the color guard saluted her and rode smartly out of the arena. She fell in behind, the box clamped tightly to her side.

Back in the schooling arena, she dismounted into the arms of her family, flashbulbs popping and several reporters asking her questions. She answered them and turned to her mom and dad. Tears had tracked down their faces, as well as the others'. Gran handed DJ a tissue, and Brad held on to Herndon's reins while DJ blew her nose.

"I never thought, I mean I . . ." DJ blew her nose again and held the box out to Gran. "Open the box, Gran."

"No, you need to." GJ took out his pocketknife and slit the tape, then the paper on the box.

In an envelope lay a check. DJ gasped and stared up at her mother. "It's for a thousand dollars to be used for tuition for college or art school."

"Wow." Shawna wore a look of total shock.

DJ knew she must look like that, too. She folded the paper back from the plaque. Sure enough, it said the same as the announcer had read, along with the date of the fire.

Horses were filing into the schooling arena.

"We better move so they can warm up," Brad said. "How about I take him back to the barn and you can talk with some of the people waiting to see you?"

"Sure, thanks." DJ looked up to realize he wasn't just talking about her family.

She didn't get back to the barn until over an hour later, and now her hands were tender from being shaken by so many people, including a certain nurse and fireman. Karen had shown DJ her engagement ring and promised to see her after the day's classes.

By the end of the day, DJ and Herndon had won one third, a fifth out of a class of thirty, and a first in Junior Hunter. Junior Jumping would begin first thing on Sunday morning.

Fifteen junior riders circled the schooling arena at 9 A.M. on Sunday. DJ had Herndon warmed up and ready; they would be jumping third, and Tony was number ten. DJ circled the ring again, all the while trying to ignore the show going on in her middle. *Calm, stay calm. Please, God, keep me calm.*

The announcer called the first rider. She trotted through the entry gate to a smattering of applause, and DJ continued around the practice ring. The announcer called a perfect round and introduced the next rider, this time a boy DJ had seen at other shows. His horse was acting up already. He knocked down a bar.

One down.

"Number three is DJ Randall riding Herndon." The applause rose, fell, and rose again as she trotted into the arena.

"Okay, big horse, let's do it." She swallowed hard as they cantered toward the first jump, a post and rail. *Three, two, one*, and they were up and over, smooth as could be and on to the next. The ten jumps disappeared beneath Herndon's flying hooves: the in and out, a brush jump, a turn and over the wall, a water jump, and a chicken coop, with a triple being the last and highest with a wide spread on the out. Herndon acted as if they'd been out playing as he cantered through the exit gate.

DJ felt like they'd conquered the world. "Thank you, God. Thank you, thank you, thank you." She threw her arms around Herndon's neck and squeezed hard. "Thank you, big horse. You're so awesome."

"DJ, did you know you're on the front page of the *San Jose Mercury News*?" Amy held up the paper with a big picture of DJ and Herndon and another of DJ accepting the plaque.

"You're in the *Sunday Chronicle*, too." Brad gave her a proud-father smile. "Way to go, kiddo."

Four entrants had jumped while she visited with her family and friends at the far corner of the ring. DJ had heard some of the announcements but not all.

Joe caught her questioning look and said, "So far three out and four in, including you."

"I better get us moving again. Talk with you later."

She moved Herndon back out into the pattern of riders and picked up a slow trot. Tony passed her. "Way to go, DJ. We're all the way."

"You just show 'em how."

When Tony finished his round, he had done just that. Another perfect score. The next round the field had narrowed to seven. The attendants raised the bars three inches and cleared the arena.

DJ jumped second this time, another perfect round following a perfect first rider. The next two hit the bars. Tony jumped a perfect round; the one following him hit; and the last one ticked—the bar rocked but didn't go down, so she was in for the next round.

With four riders left, the bars were raised another three inches, to four feet. The attendants removed one of the brush jumps and switched two others around.

Herndon cleared them all, including the direction change, with room to spare and a tail that flicked an *I told you so*. DJ had to laugh when they exited. Herndon snorted and jigged sideways as she drew him down to a walk.

This round left three riders, DJ and Tony included. The bars went up three inches again with more changes.

DJ now jumped first. When they called her number, she patted Herndon's shoulder. "This is it, big horse. They're getting high now." *Real high. Oh, Lord, please help us do our best.*

The wall looked enormous. Good thing they flew over it before DJ had time to panic. The same for the chicken coop and the brush; they all looked much higher than the others, but Herndon took each one in stride. They jumped as if they were one entity, with DJ high on his withers and Herndon with his ears pricked forward toward the next jump. They cantered out of the ring to thundering applause.

Her heart pounding, DJ accepted a bottle of water from her father. "Thanks, I needed that." She heard the crack when a horse's hoof hit a bar and the groan from the audience that told her the bar hit the dirt. "Well, he's got third place. Come on, Tony, you can do better than that."

"You want to go again?" Robert took back the half-empty bottle.

"They look awful big, huh?"

"You aren't just a-foolin'. See ya."

DJ rode out so she could keep moving. They had mountains to jump.

Tony cantered out of the ring without the fatal crack. "It's you and me, DJ, just like I said it would be."

This round they would be timed with only eight jumps and a change of direction.

While she'd never been timed competitively before, DJ felt as calm as if she'd just been riding for pleasure. She patted Herndon's neck, took in a deep breath, and let it out. They were off. Cantering smoothly, they took each jump as if they were having the time of their lives—which they were. Count, forward and lift off, sail, and touch down. At the brush she heard a tick but kept on. The bar stayed in place and they finished with a perfect round.

"Close, big horse. That was close."

Tony touched a finger to the brim of his helmet. "Don't make it easy for me."

"I didn't."

The applause told her if the lack of a hoof cracking a bar hadn't—Tony jumped a perfect round.

"These two are having too much fun out here," the announcer said. "But the bars go up to four feet, six inches with a wider spread. How high can these kids go?"

DJ wondered the same thing. Herndon grunted when he leaped for the wall, but he cleared it and snorted when he landed. DJ looked ahead and refused to panic. So what if the brush jump fell? But it didn't. They jumped a clean round again with good time.

The crowd went wild. DJ's heart raced as if to leap out of her mouth. "We did it, big horse, we did it! Thank you, Lord Jesus, we did it." Her legs felt like weak string. Her hands itched inside her gloves where the sweat had puddled.

The announcer called for Tony. A hush fell. The sound of his horse's hooves thudded through the sand. He cleared jumps one and two, then on to the next. DJ heard the crack on the third bar of the in and out, and it toppled to the ground. The crowd groaned. DJ groaned.

Tony cantered out of the ring and toward her. "You did it this time, DJ, but I'll take the next one, you just watch." His grin said he meant every word.

The crowd went wild when DJ and Tony trotted back into the arena to pick up their ribbons.

"These two do the Briones Academy proud, folks, wouldn't you say? They both train with Bridget Sommersby, and you can tell she coaches them well. DJ Randall on Herndon in first place, followed by Tony Andrada on Xavier in second. Our third place ribbon goes to . . ."

DJ didn't hear the rest. She could see her two dads jumping up and down, yelling at the top of their lungs. The rest of the family was on their feet, clapping and shouting. DJ waved and shook the hand of the presenter.

She looked at Tony. "One day the Olympics."

"You got it. The Olympics." They trotted out of the ring together.

Epilogue

DJ RANDALL LOOKED OUT over the sea of faces, the spotlights blinding her.

The higher center block held the riders from Germany, winners of the gold medal for the third time in a row. She glanced up to catch the smile of Helmut von Friedrichs. Her heart skipped a beat like it always did when he smiled at her.

Beside her on the right side, the silver side, clustered her teammates. Two points from the gold—that's all they'd missed it by. She'd done her part, though. She and her horse, His Honor, won the Grand Prix, show jumping.

The members of the French team stood on the bronze block.

Sweat trickled down DJ's back. It had been so hot, a big problem for the teams. Both horses and riders suffered from the heat and humidity, as did all the other Olympic contenders.

"Ladies and gentlemen, the medal winners of the Equestrian events."

The official hung the ribbons with gold medals around the necks of the German team, and their national anthem echoed through the stadium. DJ shifted so she could reach up and take Helmut's hand. He squeezed back, tears streaming down his face, facing forward for all the world to see.

When the music finished, the names of the Americans were called. While the list didn't include Tony Andrada or Hilary Jones, DJ knew they were both out in the crowd. She bent her neck to accept the silver medal. As she felt it settle in around her neck, she lifted her head, tears blinding her eyes, and put her shoulders back. She'd done it. They'd done it. An Olympic medal. The dream had begun as a little girl.

"Thank you, Father," she whispered. "Thank you far more than I can say."

She turned to look again at Helmut. In two weeks they would be married. Although she never would have believed it before, that gold ring was now more important to her than Olympic Gold. She felt a shiver begin in her toes and work its way up. "Way to go, God!"